She was afraid of him— or herself—as he awoke

"You shouldn't have let me fall asleep," he chided gently.

Rachel flushed. "You passed out."

Nick shook his head. "This afternoon's match and the whisky made me fall asleep. But I'm awake now," he added. "You were just about to sneak out of here, weren't you?"

Rachel wished he wouldn't hold her quite so close. "I was about to leave, yes." She began to push against him, finding his arms had tightened about her like steel bands.

"Hey, look, I'm sorry about tonight." His voice was huskily persuasive. "But I'm over it now, both the anger and the booze."

"I have to go, Nick—"

"No," he insisted forcibly. "I still need you. I don't want to be alone tonight."

CAROLE MORTIMER
is also the author of these

Harlequin Presents

Many of these books are available at your local bookseller.

For a free catalog listing all titles currently available,
send your name and address to:

HARLEQUIN READER SERVICE
1440 South Priest Drive, Tempe, AZ 85281
Canadian address: Stratford, Ontario N5A 6W2

CAROLE MORTIMER

hidden love

Harlequin Books

TORONTO • NEW YORK • LOS ANGELES • LONDON
AMSTERDAM • PARIS • SYDNEY • HAMBURG
STOCKHOLM • ATHENS • TOKYO • MILAN

For
DADDA

———————————————•———————————————

Harlequin Presents first edition April 1983
ISBN 0-373-10587-8

Original hardcover edition published in 1982
by Mills & Boon Limited

CHAPTER ONE

'RELAX, Rachel,' Danny encouraged softly, his lips nuzzling against her ear.

She was trying to, but a public park wasn't the best place for this sort of thing, even if they weren't the only couple lying on the lush green grass engaging in the same activity.

The two of them had decided to forgo the inevitable stodgy college luncheon in favour of sandwiches and a Coke sitting in the park. Their food eaten and their refuse disposed of in the nearest litter-bin, Danny had decided that kissing her would take up the fifteen minutes they had left of their lunch-hour. A few kisses were one thing, but he was getting a little too intimate for her liking.

'Danny!' She struggled to sit up.

Danny sat up too, a frown marring his youthfully handsome face. 'Rachel, don't be such a prude. I was only kissing you.'

'Yes, but—Danny . . .' she frowned, her gaze fixed on something over his shoulder. 'That woman over there,' she nodded behind him. 'She doesn't look well.'

He turned to look at the young woman too, shrugging as he turned back to Rachel. 'She's pregnant, maybe she's got cramp or something. My sister was always moaning when she had Damien.'

Having met his sister, she wasn't surprised. 'Yes, but——'

'Hey, Rachel!' he chided moodily. 'You're supposed

7

to be concentrating on me, not some very pregnant woman sitting on a park bench.' His mouth once more claimed hers.

She let him lower her back on to the grass, kissing him back, her hands entangled in the long dark hair at his nape. Any of her friends at college—with the exception of Hilary, who couldn't stand him—would gladly have taken her place, Danny being the college pin-up of the moment, very good-looking, his hair thick and dark, his eyes like brown velvet, the denims and matching denim shirt he wore skin-tight, faded with wear, giving him a rugged look that he cultivated. Yes, any number of the girls she knew at college would have taken her place, although she and Danny had been dating for two months now, meeting two or three evenings a week.

But right now she couldn't give him all of her attention, her thoughts drifting time and time again to the pale woman sitting on the bench a few feet away from them. She hadn't been there a few minutes ago, and the strained look about her mouth wouldn't be banished from Rachel's mind. She was a pretty woman, probably in her early or mid-twenties, and as Danny had already pointed out, very pregnant. It was this last fact that worried Rachel the most. What if the poor woman were about to give birth here and now?

Danny raised his head, his eyes snapping with impatience. 'Rachel, are you with me?'

'Of course.' She pushed her long dark brown hair away from her face, her long lashes the same dark colour, thickly surrounding her smoky grey eyes, her nose small and snub, covered with a light sprinkling of freckles, her mouth wide and smiling, usually. Now it was rather pensive. 'I'm just worried about that woman.' She stood up, brushing the recently cut grass from her fitted black denims and red tee-shirt, her figure boyish rather than curvaceous, her height only a little over five feet. It was because of her lack of inches, both in her figure and height, that she was often taken to be younger than her eighteen years. 'She does look ill, Danny, and——'

He stood up too, his mouth set angrily. 'She's probably just walked too far,' he dismissed callously. 'She'll be all right when she's rested for a while.'

Still Rachel hesitated. 'I think I should just see if she's okay.'

'We have to get back to college.' Danny took her hand firmly in his.

'But that woman——'

'Is probably waiting for her husband——'

'But we don't know that,' she insisted determinedly. 'It isn't going to hurt anyone if I just ask her, now is it?' the last came out almost pleadingly.

Danny angrily dropped her hand. 'Well, I'm not going to hang around while you do. I have a class in ten minutes.'

She eyed him challengingly. 'Since when did getting to a class on time bother you?'

He flushed at the taunt, suddenly only his nineteen years, his air of bravado wavering. 'It doesn't,' he said almost sulkily. 'You know that.'

'Then it isn't going to hurt you to wait two minutes while I ask her how she is, is it?' she said brightly.

'Okay,' he agreed grudgingly. 'But don't be long,' he added warningly as she turned to walk towards the other woman.

Dear Danny, he did like to think he was the Don Juan of Maddox College—and acted accordingly. When he forgot to act the macho man he could be good company, fun to be with, but in this mood he wasn't quite so pleasant.

Close to, the young woman looked even worse, a sheen of perspiration on her brow, her pale skin having a grey tinge to it, her breathing shallow and ragged.

'Excuse me . . .' Rachel began hesitantly.

The woman looked up, tears instantly flooding her eyes. 'Oh, thank God someone has actually spoken to me!' she groaned, her accent distinctly American, her hand coming out to clutch on to Rachel's. 'Can you please help me?'

Rachel sat down on the bench beside the woman. 'Of course,' she squeezed her hand reassuringly. 'Is it the baby?'

'Yes. I—I think it's going to be born soon. I've been having pains the last hour. Sharp pains,' the woman added pointedly.

Rachel chewed on her bottom lip, knowing little or nothing about giving birth. 'Do you think you should go to hospital?'

'I know so,' the other woman admitted ruefully. 'I've been trying to get out of this park and into a cab for the last thirty minutes, but no one seems willing to help.'

Rachel gave her hand another squeeze, knowing exactly what she meant, having once seen a man actually collapse in the street and people walk past him. It wasn't that the people were callous or uncaring, they just didn't want to get involved—as Danny hadn't. Only she wasn't made of the same stuff, had been the one to call an ambulance for that man and sit with him while they waited for it to arrive, and she was going to help this woman too.

'I'll help you,' she promised. 'I'll get you a taxi, and——'

'You won't leave me?' The woman sounded panicked.

'I could call someone for you——'

'Nick—he'll come. I—Oh!' she groaned, her hand squeezing the blood out of Rachel's fingers.

'A contraction?' Rachel gulped.

'Yes,' she gasped. 'They're coming quite regularly now. I don't think it can be much longer.'

Rachel was no expert, but she had the same feeling. 'There's a call-box just outside the park gates, I'll call an ambulance. And Nick.'

'Just call the ambulance,' the woman advised raggedly, pulling a tattered piece of paper out of her handbag. 'It's a private clinic,' she explained as she gave Rachel the slip of paper. 'My name is Kay Lennox, by the way—they might ask you that. The call to Nick can wait until later.'

Rachel managed to extricate her hand, flexing the fingers to recirculate the blood. 'I'll call the clinic now, and——'

'Rachel!' Danny had tired of waiting and now stood in front of them. 'We have to get back,' he hissed pointedly.

She licked her lips nervously, knowing he wasn't going to like what she said next. 'Mrs Lennox is having a baby,' she explained.

'I can see that,' he snapped.

She shook her head, and stood up. 'I mean now,' she told him softly. 'I have to call an ambulance——'

'Count me out,' he said instantly—as she had known he would. 'Rachel, you can't get involved in this!'

'I can't *not* get involved,' she snapped angrily. 'Can't you see that——'

'I can see you're determined to do this. I have a class to go to,' he told her coldly. 'Call me when you've finished—baby-sitting!' He turned and walked off.

'Danny!' She soon caught up with him, grabbing his arm to stop him. 'I thought you could stay with Mrs Lennox while I made the telephone call,' she looked up at him pleadingly.

'Then you thought wrong,' he scowled darkly. 'Are you mad, Rachel? It won't just be the telephone call, the next thing you know she'll want you to go to the hospital with her.'

'She won't ask, Danny,' her hand fell away from his arm, 'because I'll offer,' she added rebelliously.

'Then you do it alone!' He shook his head. 'You always have to interfere. Why couldn't you just leave the woman alone?'

'And let her have her baby on a park bench?' Her eyes flashed.

'She wouldn't have——'

'She still could if I don't make that call. Goodbye, Danny.'

'Rachel——'

She looked at him coldly, disappointed to find he was another of those people who didn't want to get involved. 'I said goodbye.' This time she was the one to turn and walk away.

When she next looked round it was to see Danny striding back towards the college. She doubted she would be dating him again. Oh well, maybe it was for the best; she didn't particularly like people who couldn't care for others.

She quickly called the clinic, giving them instructions on how to find them before rushing back to Kay Lennox's side. 'They'll be here in a few minutes,' she reassured her.

'Thank you.' Kay seemed to relax visibly. 'You've been so kind. The baby isn't really due for another three weeks, and I thought it would be all right for me to go shopping. Nick will be so angry when he finds out what's happened,' she frowned worriedly.

He must be a bit of a brute to be angry just because his wife was having their baby three weeks early. 'I'm sure he'll understand,' Rachel soothed softly.

'You don't know Nick,' Kay grimaced.

And she wasn't sure she wanted to! Kay seemed genuinely worried about her husband's disapproval. He should be made to understand that babies had no idea of the date picked out for them to arrive.

'I'll call him,' she promised again. 'Just as soon as we get you to the clinic. I'm sure he'll forget to be angry once he sees the baby.'

Kay grimaced once again. 'I doubt it. The last thing he said to me this morning was to take things easy.'

Rachel didn't like the sound of Nick Lennox at all, although she gave no indication of that as she accompanied the other woman to the clinic in the ambulance. Once there Kay was whisked off to a delivery room while Rachel was shown into a waiting room.

The doctor came back to tell her it would be several hours yet, and since she had tried the number Kay had given her for her husband and been met with one of those infuriating machines that said, 'I'm sorry, I'm afraid I'm out at the moment. If you wish to leave a message do so now,' she decided she had better wait here until the absent Mr Lennox came to the hospital in answer to her message for him to do so.

There were a few magazines lying about the waiting-room, but none of them really held her interest. The minutes dragged by into hours, until suddenly she realised it was almost dinner time and she had received no further word from the doctor on Kay's condition, and Nick Lennox still hadn't put in an appearance.

When she tried the telephone number Kay had given

her for a second time it was to again be met with that hollow-sounding recording, leaving the same message for Mr Lennox to come to the hospital immediately, thinking that at this rate the baby would be a year old before its father put in an appearance! It was ridiculous to leave on an answering service when you knew your wife was so near to having her baby.

The doctor came back into the waiting-room just after she had returned herself. 'No Mr Lennox yet?' he raised his eyebrows.

'I'm afraid not,' she grimaced.

'Well, in the circumstances . . . You accompanied Mrs Lennox, I believe?' he looked at her enquiringly.

'Yes,' she nodded.

He shrugged. 'It should be another hour or so before the baby is born, and Mrs Lennox keeps asking for her husband. I wondered if you would mind talking to her for a few minutes, just to assure her that he has been notified.'

The thought of entering that clinical-looking room she had caught a glimpse of as they wheeled Kay Lennox inside didn't exactly thrill her. Like most people, she had no love of hospitals. But Danny's words about getting involved came back to taunt her, and she was determined to prove to herself, if to no one else, that she could cope with this.

The gown, cap, and shoe-guards they made her wear weren't exactly glamorous, and the next few minutes of reassuring Kay that Nick had been notified and was probably on his way here even now—something she hoped, but doubted—weren't the most enjoyable she had ever spent in her life; Kay's contractions were obviously coming very frequently now.

She felt quite dizzy once she was back in the waiting-room, very grateful to the nurse who brought her a pot of tea and a sandwich. No one else had turned up in the waiting-room in her absence, so she still had the place to herself. Considering the number of babies being born in this country she was rather surprised at the small number of births in this private clinic today.

The tea was hot and strong, the chicken salad sandwich delicious, and she had just taken another mouthwatering bite when the door opened and a man came into the room. Her eyes widened as she looked at him, at the golden-blond hair, the deeply tanned skin, the obviously athletic body in the black fitted trousers and black silk shirt, the latter partly unbuttoned to reveal the darker blond hair that grew on his chest. But it was his face that was so arresting, an arrogantly handsome face that was familiar and yet somehow wasn't. His eyebrows were the same dark blond of the hair on his chest, his eyes deeply blue, the lashes long and thick, his nose long and straight, his mouth rather stern now, although the laughter lines about his eyes seemed to indicate that he didn't always look this forbidding.

Rachel slowly lowered the sandwich back on to the plate, watching with mesmerised eyes as he closed the door and walked across the room towards her, his movements made with ease, his body lean and muscled, his clothes looking good on him. He was really a very attractive man, in his late twenties or early thirties, sure of himself and other people's reaction to him.

'Miss James?'

His voice was low and husky—sexy, most of her friends would have called it. 'Yes,' she answered, frowning now. This man didn't look like a doctor. Oh, she knew that not all doctors had to wear white coats, but this man just didn't look anything like the harassed doctor who had spoken to her earlier. In fact, this man looked as if very little bothered him at all!

He nodded, as if she had just confirmed his thoughts. 'I thought so. I got your messages on my answering service, and——'

'*You're* Nick?' Her eyes widened with disbelief. *This* was Nick Lennox?

He smiled at her surprise, his eyes crinkling at the corners, as she had known they would, instantly looking more boyish, although the leashed power that surrounded him seemed to deny he had ever been that. This man looked as if he had been born experienced. 'Yes, I'm Nick,' he told her, his accent as American as his wife's, Rachel noticed for the first time.

Rachel frowned her confusion. He really wasn't what she had been expecting Kay's husband to be like. Or was it just that he didn't look like *anyone's* husband, the looks he was giving her seeming to say he didn't *feel* like anyone's husband either; open appreciation for her slender curves and gaminly attractive features were shown clearly in his deep blue eyes.

It was because of this openly flirtatious look that she answered him more sharply, more bluntly, than she might otherwise have done. 'It's about time you turned up,' she snapped. 'Do you realise I've been calling you all afternoon——'

'Twice,' he put in softly, seemingly unmoved by her attack.

She gave him an irritated look. 'Once at two-thirty, and once at five o'clock.'

'But hardly all afternoon,' he taunted.

Rachel flushed. 'That doesn't change the fact that I put in the first call over four hours ago.'

'I was out——'

'That's obvious,' she scorned.

This time he seemed to stiffen at her criticism, his eyes hardening and narrowing, his expression harsh. 'I don't have to explain my movements to you, Miss James——'

'No, you have to explain them to that poor woman in there having a baby——'

'The doctor said she's doing very well,' he frowned.

'She is. But you don't seem to have felt the need to go in and find out for yourself.' She stood up, feeling at a disadvantage being seated while he stood over her, although his extra foot in height still made her feel small and defenceless.

His mouth twisted mockingly. 'The last thing Kay needs is for me to see her in the middle of childbirth. She wouldn't thank me for it, I can assure you.'

Rachel's eyes sparkled, deeply grey in her anger. 'There's nothing wrong in seeing a woman give birth. In fact I think it's rather beautiful.'

'I'm sure it is,' he dismissed. 'Now look, Miss James, I came in here to thank you for looking after Kay, not to receive criticism from you for the fact that I happened to have been working all day, and to tell me I should go in there when I know damned well Kay wouldn't want that.'

'She's been asking for you,' she told him accusingly.

'She has?'

'Well, of course she has——'

'I don't see any "of course" about it, Miss James——'

'My name is Rachel,' she cut in impatiently. 'And of course your wife has been asking for you. Any woman would ask for her husband at such a time!'

'Ah, her husband,' he said slowly, his eyes starting to glow with amusement. 'Yes, I suppose a husband would be wanted at such a time.' His arms were folded across his broad chest, the cuffs of his shirt sleeves turned back to just below his elbow, a plain gold watch fastened about his right wrist. 'But you see,' he added mockingly, 'I'm not Kay's husband.'

'I—You aren't?' Rachel gasped.

'Nope,' he answered confidently, those deep blue eyes sweeping over her with deepening amusement.

She frowned. 'But she asked for you.'

'Yes,' he nodded, 'I'm sure she did.'

She had been so sure Nick was Kay's husband, was sure the doctor had thought so too. But then she hadn't really noticed whether or not Kay Lennox was wearing a wedding ring, and she hadn't asked *specifically* for her husband, just for Nick. Well, if he wasn't her husband he must be . . . Her mouth twisted as she looked at his arrogantly confident face, the mocking smile as she began to blush.

Heaven knew she wasn't a prude, the permissive society had been going on long before she was even born, but surely there were enough illegitimate children in the world already without adding to their number.

'I'm sorry,' her voice was stiff with disapproval, 'I didn't realise you weren't married.'

Nick moved to one of the armchairs and sat down, the ankle of one leg resting on the knee of the other one, looking completely relaxed as he smiled up at her. 'I'm not—but Kay is,' he informed her softly.

Goodness, this was getting more and more complicated! Nick wasn't Kay's husband, but she did have one somewhere. And was the baby Nick's or her husband's?

'Before your imagination runs riot,' he taunted, the blue eyes narrowed, 'I think maybe I should tell you that I'm Kay's adopted brother.'

'Her—her brother?' Rachel gulped.

'Yes.'

What an idiot he must think her! Although in all honesty he had done nothing to correct her obvious misunderstanding, had known what she was thinking and had made no effort to acquaint her with the truth. This Nick—aptly named as far as she was concerned!—had been having fun at her expense. How ridiculous she must have looked when she tried to reprove him about not being married when he was expecting to be a father at any minute!

Her head went back, her stature challenging, her eyes flashing deeply grey as her hair fell straight and gleaming to her waist, mahogany-dark, a startling contrast to her red tee-shirt. 'Very funny,' she snapped, gathering up the books she had brought with her, intending to have taken them to her next class. 'I'll leave now you're here.'

He moved with a speed that surprised her and was standing at her side even as she pressed the books to her breasts. He grasped one of her wrists. 'Don't go,' he said huskily, the pressure on her narrow wrist unsettling the books she was holding and causing several of them to crash to the floor. 'Sorry.' He released her, bending to pick up the books, the overhead lighting making his hair look like gold.

Rachel stood in shocked silence, waiting for the wild sensations from her wrist to the rest of her body to stop. Her skin actually tingled where he had touched her, although there were no visible marks there to tell her just why this man's touch made her feel so odd.

He was straightening now, giving her chalky-coloured cheeks a quizzical look, the clear blue of his eyes like a Mediterranean sea. 'Hey, I didn't hurt you, did I?' he queried softly, standing so close she could see the green speckles in the blue of his eyes, could smell the spicy cologne he wore, the male warmth of his body.

She quivered as sexual attraction gripped her, a sensation such as she had never known before, a feeling of wanting to press herself against this man and be engulfed by him. It was mad, utterly out of character, and yet as soon as he had entered the room she had been totally aware of him. That was maybe even the reason she had been so sharp with him when she thought he was Kay's husband.

He was looking at her now, the brooding blue eyes puzzled, a frown marring his brow. And well he might. He was probably wondering what was wrong with her, he had spoken to her several minutes ago and she hadn't answered him yet.

She licked her suddenly dry lips, aware that to this ultra-sophisticated man she must appear very juvenile. Especially now, when she was acting like an infatuated teenager instead of a responsible eighteen-year-old. 'No, you didn't hurt me,' she answered strongly. 'One of the books fell on my toe,' she invented.

'Mm,' he looked down at the title of one of them. 'They look heavy—in more ways than one.'

'They are.' She snatched the books out of his hands—taking care not to touch him again, putting them on top of the others.

'*Business in the Eighties*,' he quoted softly. 'Rather a strange subject for a schoolgirl to be studying, isn't it?'

'I'm not a schoolgirl, Mr—er——'

'Nick,' he invited softly.

Rachel flushed. 'I'm not a schoolgirl,' she repeated, this time omitting to call him anything. 'I'm at college. And I'm doing a business course.'

'And you missed classes this afternoon to bring my sister to hospital?'

'Yes.'

'We're very grateful to you,' he said deeply.

'I didn't do it for gratitude,' she snapped, still too raw from that strange reaction she had had to him. 'Your sister, Mrs Lennox, was obviously in need of help.'

'Nevertheless——'

'I really have to go now.' She looked away from him, unnerved by his steady look. 'I have a class this evening.'

His dark blond eyebrows rose. 'In the evenings too?'

'I take languages at night, French and German.'

'Do you have time for a social life?'

'Of course,' she flashed.

The door opened and the doctor came into the room. 'Your sister would like to see you for a few minutes,' he spoke to Nick.

Nick hesitated. 'Is it all right?'

'Just for a few minutes,' the other man nodded.

Nick looked at Rachel. 'You'll wait for me?'

'Wait for me'—how casually those words were spoken, and yet Rachel had the strangest feeling that if he had said them seriously, with the intention of coming back to her no matter what stood in his way of their being together, her answer would have been the same. 'Yes,' she told him huskily.

Seconds after he had left the room she was wondering why she was still here. She had done her good deed for the day, had got Kay Lennox to the hospital, her brother was now here to keep her company, so there was no reason for her to stay any longer. Except Nick's request that she 'wait for him'.

It was stupid, utterly insane. She should be on her way to her French class, not sitting here waiting for a man she had just met, a man who seemed altogether too confident of his attraction to women. She didn't doubt there had been plenty of them in his life, the light of experience in his eyes seemed to say there had been many.

She knew all that, knew there was just no valid reason for her to stay here, and yet she was still sitting in the waiting-room when Nick returned.

He was pale beneath his tan, sinking gratefully into the nearest chair. 'Do you think all women have to go through that?'

'You mean you don't know?' she asked bitchily, frightened of her own reaction to this man, feeling his magnetism even stronger the second time around.

'I told you, I'm not married.'

'That doesn't preclude your having a child,' she said insultingly.

If anything he paled even more, this time with anger. 'It does in my book,' he ground out. 'Any child of mine will know my love, my full-time love—unlike my own parents, who didn't give a damn.'

'Where is your sister's husband?' asked Rachel.

'In New York on business. He left Kay in my care.'

The look she gave him showed him what she thought of his way of looking after his sister.

His eyes hardened. 'She wasn't supposed to have gone out,' he said abruptly.

'She said she wanted to do some shopping.'

Nick nodded. 'Clothes for the baby—as if she doesn't have enough. I don't suppose she had you call Richard?'

'In New York?' she scorned.

'No, I suppose not,' he sighed. 'Then I'd better do that now.'

'I'll go——'

'No, wait. Please,' he added at her rebellious look. 'The doctor said it won't be long at all now, so you may as well wait and see what she has. You never know,' he added mockingly, 'if it's a girl she may decide to name it after you. Raquel, you said?'

'Rachel,' she corrected irritably.

'Okay, Rachel,' he taunted. 'You might as well wait and see whether it's a boy or a girl. If it isn't too late I'll drive you to your class afterwards.'

Her mouth twisted. 'It's already too late. It began five minutes ago,' she explained.

'I'm sorry.'

'It doesn't matter. I have the books, I can probably do the lesson at home.'

'Intelligent as well as beautiful!'

Rachel tried her hardest not to blush, but knew she hadn't succeeded when she saw the satisfaction in his eyes. He knew exactly what sort of effect he was having on her—and he was enjoying the fact. He would probably tell his equally sophisticated girl-friend all about the gauche young girl he had met today when next they met. She knew he would have a girl-friend, a woman he went to bed with; the air of sensuality that surrounded him must be satisfied by some one.

'Your telephone call,' she reminded him stiffly.

'Mm.' He stood up, each movement he made fluidly co-ordinated. 'Is there anyone you have to let know where you are?'

Rachel shook her head, her dark hair swinging forward. 'I called my parents earlier and told them to expect me when they see me.'

'I'll drive you home later. Right now I'd better let Richard know he's about to be a father three weeks early.' Nick grimaced. 'He'll be so damned mad—at himself,' he added at Rachel's raised eyebrows. 'He didn't want to go on this business trip, but Kay persuaded him to go against his better judgment. He should have known better than to trust my sister, she's never been on time for anything in her life, although she's usually late.'

An unwilling smile curved her lips, her teeth small and pearly white, two tiny dimples appearing in her cheeks.

Nick's eyes widened as he looked at her, almost as if he were seeing her for the first time. 'I'll go and make that call,' he muttered, leaving the room.

Rachel was left with that 'kicked in the stomach' feeling again. Nick was like no other man she had ever met, and she acted like a nervous schoolgirl every time he so much as looked at her.

Except when she had made that bitchy comment about him possibly being a father, and he hadn't liked that at all, his reaction against that had been very strong. Maybe she should apologise? But if she did that she would be making an issue out of it. Better to just forget the subject.

She gave him a warm smile when he returned a few minutes later. 'Did you manage to speak to your brother-in-law?' she asked.

'Yes.' Nick closed the door. 'He's getting the first plane back. He's a bit annoyed because he wanted to be with Kay at the birth, but I told him he wasn't missing much.'

Rachel gave a light laugh, her eyes a deep grey. 'I gather you don't intend being present when you marry and your wife has a baby.'

'That depends,' he drawled.

'On what?'

'On whether this imaginary wife wants me there.'

'Oh,' she blushed. 'Of course.'

They both looked up as the door was opened, and looked anxiously at the doctor, relaxing as he beamed at them. 'Mrs Lennox has a lovely little girl,' he announced. 'Seven pounds four ounces.'

Nick swallowed hard. 'Are they both all right?'

'Yes,' the doctor still smiled. 'Mrs Lennox is very tired, but she would like to see you both before we take her to her room.'

Rachel let Nick hold her elbow as they went in to see the tired but ecstatic new mother, the tiny shawl-wrapped baby she cradled in her arms already fast asleep.

'Isn't she beautiful?' she glowed up at her brother.

He looked down at the tiny red-faced baby, honesty obviously warring with brotherly love. The latter won. 'Yes, she's lovely, honey,' he squeezed his sister's hand. 'Beautiful, just like you.'

'Rachel,' Kay turned to look at her, 'thank you so much for all that you did for me, calling Nick and everything. Even if he was late getting here,' she added teasingly.

'I was at the court all day, Kay. I had no idea I was going to be needed.'

'Excuses, excuses!' she said mischievously.

Rachel was still taking in the fact that Nick was a lawyer. He didn't look anything like she had imagined a lawyer to look, like the lawyers they portrayed on television. Maybe in one of those formal suits they wore . . .? No, he just didn't fit the part.

'Time for you to rest now,' he was telling his sister. 'I'll be back to see you tomorrow. Richard should be back by then too. Right now I'm going to take Rachel out to celebrate the birth of my new niece.'

'Oh, I——'

'Going to wet the baby's head?' Kay teased.

'Something like that.' He gave a soft laugh, his hand still firm on Rachel's elbow. 'Take care, honey. And give my new niece a kiss from me when she wakes up.'

'When she's older I'll tell her how brave her uncle was at her birth,' Kay's eyes twinkled with humour.

'Time to go now,' the nurse told them softly, taking the baby and putting her in the waiting cot.

Rachel collected her books from the waiting-room before accompanying Nick outside. 'I really can't go for a drink with you,' she repeated the refusal he had interrupted in his sister's room.

'You aren't under age, are you?'

'No,' she flushed. 'I'm eighteen. I just have to get home and read up tomorrow's classes.'

'Has anyone ever told you you work too hard?'

Danny had, frequently. But she was determined to do well in this business course; she didn't want to remain just a secretary when she left college at the end of next year but to make a viable career for herself in the world of business.

'I'm really very grateful for the offer, but——'

'But you still refuse.' They were walking across the car park now, Nick leading her to the side of a sleek Jaguar, its red colour visible to her in the bright evening light.

Rachel's eyes opened wide with appreciation as he unlocked the passenger door for her. Being a lawyer must pay well! 'I have to refuse. As you said, those books are heavy going, and I always read the appropriate chapter for the next day's classes the evening before.'

'Very conscientious,' he taunted. 'In you get,' he encouraged.

Rachel climbed into the low seat, the car perfectly matching its owner, sleek and powerful. As Nick slid into the seat beside her she was instantly aware of the intimacy of the inside of the car, Nick's electricity was a tangible thing. She was pleased and flattered that such a man wanted her to share in his celebration, but it just wasn't possible.

'I'm sorry,' she muttered as he flicked the ignition, the engine purring into life.

'Do you have night school tomorrow?' he asked.

'Tomorrow?' she blinked at him.

'Hmm,' he nodded as he manoeuvred the car out into the traffic. 'We could celebrate tomorrow if you aren't busy.'

'Won't you be visiting your sister?'

'Not all evening. Richard should be back by then anyway.'

She was tempted—how she was tempted! And why not? A drink and a chat, what harm could it do? Besides, a man like this couldn't possibly have any real romantic interest in her. No, his invitation was just another thank-you for helping his sister. 'Then I'd like to come for a drink,' she accepted shyly.

'And dinner?'

She gave a happy laugh. 'And dinner. Thank you.'

'Fine. Now you'd better direct me to your home, we can't keep driving around all night,' he mocked lightly.

She gave him the directions, relaxing back in her seat as he put on a Barbra Streisand cassette. She shot him the occasional sideways glance, hardly able to believe he was going to take her out to dinner tomorrow. With his expensive elegance she would have to review the contents of her wardrobe. Maybe she shouldn't have agreed to dinner, she really didn't have anything to wear, and——

'We're here,' Nick prompted softly.

'Oh!' She looked out of the window, seeing the dearly familiar house she had lived in all of her life.

'Oh yes. Well, thank you,' and she opened the door, turning to get out.

Nick's hand on her arm stopped her. 'Eight o'clock tomorrow?'

'Er—Fine.' The temptation to spend an evening in the company of this man was just too much. 'Goodnight.'

He leant forward, kissing her lightly on the mouth. 'Goodnight, Rachel. I really am grateful to you for helping Kay.'

She blushed, lightly as the kiss had been given. Could it be that he didn't see her as a schoolgirl after all? 'Then I'll have to make sure I choose an expensive dinner, won't I?' she said cheekily.

Nick's throaty chuckle showed he appreciated her humour, and she turned and waved to him before going into the house, leaning weakly back against the door. This morning, even this afternoon, she hadn't even met him, and now she was looking forward to her date with him tomorrow.

As she went into the sitting-room she wondered what her parents would make of him. They were watching the late evening news as she came in, her mother plump and homely as she knitted a jumper for a neighbour's child, her father intent on the world events of the day. They were nice ordinary people, and she loved them very much, but she was aware that Nick was anything but ordinary. He was like an electric charge to the system, full of forceful energy, with a lazy charm that captivated.

'Boy or girl?' her mother asked softly as she sat down beside her on the sofa.

Her father gave her a vague look, his affection evident in his smile. 'Hello, love.'

'Dad,' she answered in a hushed voice, knowing she

wasn't to talk any louder until the news and weather had finished. 'It was a girl, Mum,' she answered the query. 'I hadn't realised newborn babies were so tiny.' She had been awestruck at the miniature perfection of the baby's hands and feet, her thick thatch of golden hair.

'You were beautiful when you were born,' her mother said dreamily. 'You were premature, only five and a half pounds in weight, and premature babies are always prettier. Why, what are you smiling at, Rachel?'

Her humour deepened. 'I was just thinking of the baby's uncle's reaction when he first saw her. She was all screwed up and wrinkled, and yet her mother was convinced she was beautiful.' And to Nick's credit he hadn't shown by so much as a blink of an eyelid that he didn't apprecite the baby's looks.

'The baby's uncle, dear?' her mother prompted.

'Yes. Mrs Lennox's husband was away, so I—Dad, what is this?' she asked sharply, something, some-one on the television catching and holding her attention.

'Hmm?'

'What are they talking about?' she repeated impatiently.

'Why, the tennis, of course,' he answered with equal impatience. It was *obvious* what they were talking about, with two men fiercely hitting the ball at each other, determination on each of their faces.

'What tennis?' she asked agitatedly, desperately trying to come to grips with something that was becoming more and more obvious by the second.

'Wimbledon, dear,' it was her mother who answered this time. 'They played the quarter-finals today.'

And the man playing in one of them was none other

than Kay Lennox's brother Nick! No wonder he had seemed so familiar, she had actually watched him playing one of the qualifying matches earlier in the week, had sat and cheered him on.

He was Nicholas St Clare, world-famous tennis player, winner of numerous tournaments the last twelve years, since he had turned professional at the age of eighteen. And the court he had been talking about this evening hadn't been a court of law but a tennis court, a tennis court at the world-renowned Wimbledon Championship!

CHAPTER TWO

SHE had calmly agreed to go to dinner with a famous tennis player! Of course she hadn't known who he was then, but she knew now! He was one of the hot-shot left-handed players to come out of America the last fifteen years, and at thirty years of age he was being compared with the stamina and skill of Australia's Rod Laver, was still winning the titles, although it was a well-known fact that Bjorn Borg and John McEnroe had dominated the courts of Wimbledon for the past six or seven years. Apparently it was a championship Nicholas St Clare coveted, and this year he was determined to win.

The way he had played today, by the look of the television coverage, he could just do it too. In the white shorts and short-sleeved tee-shirt he looked handsomer than ever, his golden hair clinging damply to his forehead, his blue eyes steely as he concentrated completely on winning the match from his opponent.

'Did he win?' Rachel asked breathlessly.

'I don't know who you mean by he,' her father told her. 'But Nicholas St Clare won, quite easily as a matter of fact.'

Of course he had won, he would hardly have been in that lazily charming mood otherwise. But she had agreed to have dinner with a good-looking man named Nick, not with Nicholas St Clare. She couldn't go out with a man as famous as that. And she couldn't imagine why he had asked her!

'Danny called,' her mother interrupted her panicked thoughts.

'He did?' she frowned. She had forgotten all about Danny during the last few hours!

'He seemed quite surprised you were still at the hospital.'

'He was surprised I went at all,' Rachel remembered angrily. 'If he'd had his way Mrs Lennox would have been left to fend for herself!'

'Oh dear!' her mother frowned, having the same dark hair as Rachel, although it was kept short and curly. 'Have the two of you argued?'

'Not exactly,' she avoided, her mind racing on as to how she could get in touch with Nick St Clare and tell him she couldn't go out with him tomorrow or any other time. She could call him, she had his number, but unless she got that impersonal answering service she didn't want to do that. She certainly didn't want to talk to Nick himself!

'How not exactly, Rachel?' her mother was concerned. 'I thought you were—fond of him?'

'I was—I am. But he wasn't very understanding about poor Mrs Lennox.' The only thing to do seemed to have Nick's sister pass on a message to him.

Her mother smiled. 'Men never are, dear. They have no idea.'

Nick St Clare had had no idea, he had been visibly shaken by what his sister was going through to give birth to her daughter. *Nick St Clare . . .*! Oh, she should have recognised him, should have known who he was. She just hadn't been expecting to see a famous tennis-player, and so she hadn't; she had even thought he could be a lawyer!

She had made a mess of things, and first thing tomorrow she would get herself out of it. Nick had said he would be visiting his sister some time tomorrow and so she could be sure he would get the message.

As she lay in bed later that night she did her best to convince herself that she was doing the right thing, the only thing, by not meeting Nick again. A man like that could turn her life so upside down it would never be the same again. And boring as it might appear to him, she liked her little world, was enjoying this two-year course at college, and she loved her parents very much, as their only child she felt cherished and loved in return, and she enjoyed going out on the occasional date with boys like Danny. Yes, her life was good, satisfying, and she didn't need the sophistication of Nick St Clare to spoil it all.

But hadn't he spoilt it already? Hadn't meeting him at all made her long for something she could never have? Hadn't it made her want Nick St Clare himself?

She buried her head beneath the pillow, pushing such tortuous thoughts from her mind. She *couldn't* see Nick St Clare again, and that was that.

Kay Lennox was sleeping when she telephoned from college early next morning, so she left a message with the nurse for Kay to pass on to her brother.

She slipped quietly into her place for her first class before Mr Balfour walked in to give the lecture.

'What happened to you yesterday afternoon?' Hilary leant over to whisper.

Rachel and Hilary had become friends the previous September when they had turned out to be the only two girls in this male-orientated class, but she shook her head at her friend as Mr Balfour came into the room. 'I'll tell you later,' she promised, feeling as if she would burst if she didn't soon tell someone about her meeting with Nick St Clare.

Hilary was incredulous as they ate a doughnut and

drank coffee during the morning break. 'You're joking!' Her eyes were agog, laughing blue eyes, her hair kept short and boyish.

'I wish I were,' Rachel grimaced.

'You don't!'

'Of course I do.' She stared mournfully into her rapidly cooling coffee. 'I spoke to him as if he were just like you and me. I was even cheeky to him a couple of times.'

'Being a famous tennis player doesn't make him different from the rest of us,' her friend teased.

Rachel pulled a face. 'You didn't meet him. He—well, he's magnetic, has this leashed power . . .' She shrugged. 'He is different, Hilary, believe me.'

'I can see he is,' her friend soothed. 'But he can't have minded the way you spoke to him, otherwise he wouldn't have asked you out.'

'I told you, that was just out of gratitude.'

'Some gratitude!' Hilary scorned. 'Flowers or a box of chocolates would have sufficed as far as gratitude goes. No, Nick St Clare really wanted you to go out with him.'

'That's silly, Hilary——'

'I doubt if Danny will think so.'

'Danny?' Rachel frowned.

'Danny,' Hilary nodded, looking pointedly over Rachel's shoulder.

She turned with a groan, seeing Danny making his way determinedly to their table. And he didn't look very happy, far from it in fact.

'Hilary,' he nodded tersely in her direction.

'Danny,' she greeted in a tight voice. Danny Maxwell was not one of her favourite people, something he was only too well aware of.

'Can I talk to you, Rachel?' he asked tightly.

She flushed. 'Well I——'

'Don't mind me.' Hilary stood up, as slender as Rachel but slightly taller. She picked up her cup. 'I want to get a refill anyway. Rachel?'

'Not for me, thanks,' she refused, watching as Danny sat down in Hilary's vacated chair. 'That wasn't very kind,' she told him sharply.

'I'm not feeling particularly kind,' he scowled. 'Did your mother tell you I telephoned last night?'

'Yes,' she nodded.

His eyes narrowed. 'But you didn't feel like calling me back?'

'I got home late, Danny——'

'From taking that woman to hospital?'

'Yes. You see——'

'I told you you'd get dragged into being in-volved——'

'I didn't get dragged into anything, Danny,' she sighed. 'I stayed with her because I wanted to. She had a little girl, if you're interested.'

'I'm not,' he said coldly.

'I didn't think you would be.'

'And what's that supposed to mean?' He was instantly on the defensive.

'Nothing,' she muttered, gathering her books together. 'I have to get to my next class.'

His hand on her wrist stopped her, but there was none of the tingling sensation she had experienced with Nick St Clare. 'Is our date for tonight still on?'

She had forgotten all about their arrangements to go and see the latest James Bond film. But she didn't want to go anyway, she found Danny's behaviour of yesterday had put her off the boy himself. 'Not tonight, Danny——'

'Why?'

'I—Well, because——'

'You don't want to see me any more, right?' he said roughly.

Oh dear, she always hated breaking up with boys, especially as Danny didn't appear to be going to make it easy for her; his grip on her wrist was unrelenting. 'I think it might be better if——'

'Oh, spare me the little speech about how you don't want to see me any more but we can still be friends,' he sneered, releasing her wrist. 'I've said it too many times myself to know it isn't true.'

'Danny, I'm sorry——'

'I'm not,' he said insultingly. 'You're a little prude, Rachel. I think two months is long enough to tell me you aren't going to give me anything but kisses.'

She flushed. 'Is that all you can think about, what you can get from a girl?'

His mouth twisted mockingly, marring his good looks. 'What else is there?' he scorned. 'You surely didn't think I intended getting serious about you?'

'I hope not,' she told him with blunt honesty, standing up to look down at him with cold grey eyes. 'I think you have a lot of growing up to do before you become serious about anyone.'

'Ready, Rachel?' Hilary appeared at her side.

Rachel looked down at Danny's angrily flushed face, flicking her hair back. 'More than ready,' she nodded, leaving with her friend.

Hilary giggled as they stepped into the lift. 'What did you say to upset him?'

'Just the truth,' she shrugged. 'That I didn't want to go out with him any more.'

'You finished with Danny Maxwell?' her friend gasped.

'Well . . . yes.'

'You really did?' Hilary frowned.

'Yes.'

'Goodness!'

'Well, don't sound so surprised,' Rachel laughed. 'It isn't unheard-of, you know.'

'To Danny Maxwell it is!'

'Not any more,' she grinned, feeling no remorse. Danny had been as surprised as Hilary by her decision not to see him any more, and his reaction had shown him in his true colours.

'I'm glad,' Hilary said seriously. 'I never did like him. He's all tight jeans and biceps.'

'Hilary!'

'Well, he is,' her friend muttered. 'Now Nicholas St Clare is what I would call a real man.'

Rachel stiffened, glad that the lift had arrived at their floor. 'I don't want to talk about Mr St Clare.'

'But——'

'Hilary!' she said in a warning voice.

'Well, I think you're mad. Even if you never saw him again you would at least have had this one evening to remember.'

She knew that, that one thought had been going through her mind all morning. Maybe she should have just had this one date with him. But what good would it do? He was probably another one of those men who weren't interested if he couldn't have more than kisses.

'I'm not interested,' she told Hilary firmly.

The rest of the day seemed to drag to Rachel, and for once she wasn't giving her whole attention to her work, something one of the tutors warned her about.

'Do you want to come over tonight?' Hilary offered. 'We could play a few records, chat, you know.'

'I know,' Rachel pulled a face. 'You only want to try and get my innermost secrets out of me.'

'How did you guess?' her friend grinned.

She laughed. 'It wasn't difficult. Thanks for the offer, Hilary, but I have to wash my hair.'

Hilary looked admiringly at the long dark tresses. 'I bet it takes all evening, hmm?'

'More or less. My mother usually brushes it dry for me. It takes hours.'

'Your poor mother!'

Rachel grinned. 'I tell her it's the price she has to pay for my growing it this long.'

Hilary touched her own boyishly styled hair. 'I sometimes wish I hadn't had mine cut, but when I hear I'd have to waste an evening just washing and drying hair your length I'm glad mine only takes half an hour to wash and dry.'

'It has its benefits,' Rachel agreed.

'It does?'

'Hm, it fills an empty evening.' And it looked as if she would be having a lot of them in the near future.

Hilary shook her head. 'And you could have filled this one with Nick St Clare, not a shampoo bottle.'

'Hilary, I'd rather——'

'Well, well, well,' drawled an insulting voice. 'If it isn't the little girl that likes to date tennis stars!'

Rachel turned to face Danny, finding he had two of his friends with him. Billy and Malcolm were nice enough boys on their own, but Danny was obviously their leader, and they were following his lead in this, their expressions as mocking.

'I don't know where you got your information——'

'Why, your little friend here.' Danny's gaze strayed to Hilary. 'She's full of the fact that her best friend is going out with Nick St Clare.'

Rachel looked at her friend, knowing by her flushed

cheeks that Danny spoke the truth. 'Hilary!' she groaned.

'I'm sorry,' the other girl looked at her appealingly.

'No wonder you aren't interested in going out with me any more,' Danny scorned. 'Some hot-shot with a lot of money comes along and I'm no longer good enough for you.'

'It wasn't like that,' Rachel flushed. 'I——'

'Rachel?'

She instantly paled, turning at the sound of that familiar drawl, her eyes widening as she looked at Nicholas St Clare. He was standing only a couple of feet away from them, the dark brown shirt stretching tautly across his chest and shoulders, partly unbuttoned, the sleeves turned back to just below his elbows, the cream trousers fitted to his muscular thighs.

Danny's stance instantly became challenging. 'How nice,' he taunted. 'Your *boy friend* has come to pick you up from school!'

Rachel gave him a distressed look, and she heard Hilary gasp at her side. Nick looked unmoved, eyeing the younger man with amusement. She had no idea what he was doing here, or even *how* he had got here. She didn't remember telling him what time she finished, or even what college she attended. 'Ready?' she repeated dazedly.

'I told your mother and father I'd take you straight home,' he further astounded her by announcing.

She swallowed hard, still not understanding, but getting his message that he was here to drive her home. She could see the Jaguar parked a short distance away, although with the hostile audience they had it could seem like a mile.

'You haven't forgotten?' he prompted, his eyes narrowed.

'I—er—No, of course not. 'Bye, Danny, boys.' She couldn't quite look at any of them.

'Would your friend like a lift home?' Nick offered as she reached his side.

She had forgotten all about poor Hilary, although in the circumstances perhaps that wasn't so surprising. 'Hilary?' she asked softly, almost pleadingly.

Hilary's awed gaze hadn't left Nick St Clare since he had first spoken, and she had some difficulty answering Rachel. 'Er—no—thanks,' she finally managed to stutter. 'I have some shopping to do.'

Rachel knew the other girl must be completely bowled over, otherwise she would never have refused!

'I'll see you tomorrow, Rachel,' Danny put in softly, obviously still out to cause trouble.

'Probably,' she answered coolly. 'The college isn't that big.'

'Goodbye,' Nick said generally, his hand firm on Rachel's elbow, and guided her over to the Jaguar, opening the passenger door with a flourish.

She daren't look in Danny's direction as the car moved away from the kerbside, knowing she would see contempt in his face if she did.

'I gather he's a friend of yours?' Nick spoke abruptly.

Her lashes fluttered nervously as she looked at him, the realisation of seeing him once again washing over her. His presence outside the college really had come as a surprise to her, so much so that it hadn't occured to her to protest when he told her he was driving her home. It had almost been as if she had no mind of her own.

'He was,' she answered huskily.

'Was?' Nick prompted.

'Yes,' she almost snapped her reply.

'He wouldn't happen to be the boy you were kissing

in the park yesterday, would he?' Nick taunted.

Colour flooded her cheeks. She hadn't realised Kay Lennox had seen her with Danny, but she was the only one who could have passed on such information to Nick St Clare. Had she also passed on her message to him?

'I can see he was.' Nick's eyes mocked her as he glanced at her, the rush-hour traffic holding most of his attention. 'Don't you know there are more private places for making love?'

Rachel flushed, with anger this time. 'We weren't making love, we were kissing! And it's none of your business where I do it.'

'It might be if I were the man you were kissing,' he said softly.

His words robbed her of speech, as they were supposed to, she felt sure. She had pushed the memory of the light kiss he had given her last night to the back of her mind, but now the thrill just that fleeting touch of his lips had given her came flooding back.

'Did your sister give you my message?' she asked to cover her embarrassment.

Nick glanced at her. 'That you couldn't make dinner tonight?'

'Yes,' she nodded.

'Yes, she gave it to me.'

Rachel frowned her consternation. 'Then why are you here?'

'To take you home. Your mother said you usually finish about this time——'

'When did you see my mother?' she asked sharply.

'About an hour ago.'

'But—I—You——'

Nick chuckled softly. 'Did you want to say something, Rachel?'

'Yes, I did!' she snapped. 'What are you *doing* here?'

He sighed. 'I just told you——'

'You didn't tell me anything,' she flashed. 'If your sister passed on my message that I couldn't meet you tonight then why did you go to my home?'

'To give you the flowers.'

'What flowers?' She was becoming really agitated now, and Nick's annoying attitude did not help.

'I don't know,' he shrugged. 'I didn't make a list of the different varieties.'

'Nick!'

'Hmm?'

'Oh, I give up!' She subsided into her seat. 'You're impossible!' She contented herself with glaring at the perfection of his profile.

'So I've often been told,' he shrugged.

'It's true!'

'Rachel,' he was serious now, the teasing had left his eyes, his mouth was no longer smiling, 'why did you call off our date?'

'I—You——'

'I don't remember you stuttering like this last night,' he frowned.

'When we spoke last night I had no idea you were Nicholas St Clare!' She fidgeted with her tee-shirt, pulling it down over her denims.

'But now you do.'

'Yes, now I do!'

'And you no longer want to go out with me?'

'No.'

'Why?'

She had been hoping he wouldn't ask that. 'I—Well, because of who you are, I suppose. When I got home I saw you on the television——'

'A bit of a shock for you,' he said dryly.

'Yes. Congratulations on the win, by the way,' she mumbled.

'Thanks,' he drawled. 'But I usually like to win with women too.'

She could imagine he did; she had often seen photographs of him in the newspapers with beautiful women—which made his wanting to take her out all the more unbelievable.

'I'm not in any competition,' she told him firmly. 'If I'd known who you were yesterday I would never have accepted.'

'But having accepted, it isn't polite to back out now.'

'I'm not backing out——' she began.

'You are.'

'No, I——'

'Rachel,' he spoke her name softly, but he instantly had her attention. 'I'm taking you out to dinner.'

'But——'

'No more arguments.'

'Have you always been spoilt?' she asked moodily.

'No,' he answered somewhat grimly. 'Which is why I like my own way now.'

She frowned. 'My parents—what did you say to them?'

'Nothing outrageous, I can assure you,' he mocked, pulling the car over to the side of the road, ignoring the 'No parking' sign as he turned to look at her. 'Richard wanted to send you some flowers for helping bring his daughter safely into the world, so I told him I would deliver them in person, and when you weren't home your mother gave me directions to the college. That's all there was to it.'

Her mother was an ardent tennis fan, never missed any of Wimbledon, and Rachel doubted she had taken the arrival of Nicholas St Clare on her doorstep with the calm Nick thought she had. Her poor mother was probably in a complete panic by this time!

'Rachel?' Nick gently touched her cheek.

She looked up at him with wide grey eyes, her lashes long and thick, her face completely bare of make-up; she did not even wear lip-gloss to college. 'Why did you decide to bring the flowers yourself?' she asked huskily.

His eyes deepened in colour, fixed on the parted softness of her mouth. 'I think we both know the answer to that,' he murmured.

Her lashes fluttered nervously. 'We do?'

Nick nodded, suddenly so close his warm breath stirred the hair at her temple. 'Did you know that your mouth tastes like honey?' he said throatily, his thumb-tip caressing her lips.

It was as if they were in a world of their own, the roar of the passing traffic, the rush and bustle of the pedestrians all ceasing to exist, all the world, all the reality she needed, right here in Nick's eyes.

His head lowered and his mouth claimed hers, parting her lips with the tip of his tongue as he felt her complete surrender. That dizzy pleasure that she had felt only fleetingly the night before came back tenfold, and her hands clung weakly to his shirt-front as he plundered her mouth with deeper intensity.

At last he raised his head, his eyes the colour of a stormy ocean, his breathing as ragged as her own. 'Pure nectar,' he murmured huskily.

Rachel gazed up at him with stars in her eyes. 'Nick . . .?'

'Yes,' he breathed deeply. 'Explosive, aren't we? Still refuse to have dinner with me?'

At that moment she could have denied him nothing,

although luckily he was asking for nothing but dinner. She forgot to be frightened of who he was, forgot her apprehension as to how long he would want her in his life, remembering only that together they *were* explosive.

If her parents were at all surprised to have Nicholas St Clare sitting in their lounge waiting for their daughter to change to go out to dinner with him then they didn't show it, her mother offering him a cup of tea, her father offering him the newspaper he hadn't even read himself yet.

Rachel floated up to her bedroom, having duly admired the beautiful bouquet her mother was arranging in vases for her. The accompanying card contained the sincere thanks of Richard Lennox.

She really didn't have a lot in her wardrobe that was suitable for dinner with Nick, although he had warned her it would be a quiet and early dinner, as the semi-finals tomorrow meant he had to get plenty of sleep tonight. She had a silky shirtwaister dress that would be suitable for a quiet dinner for two, its muted shade of grey matching the colour of her eyes, and darkening her hair to ebony. She could see Nick approved of her appearance when she entered the lounge a few minutes later; he stood up as she entered the room, having eyes only for her.

She blushed at that look, breaking into speech about how beautiful the flowers looked in the three vases it had taken to hold them all. 'I hope you'll thank your brother-in-law for me,' she said shyly.

His mouth quirked into a smile. 'At this rate it could take a lifetime to pass your thanks backwards and forwards to each other!'

A lifetime? Yes, she would like that.

'Do you mind if we go back to my apartment first?'

he asked once they had taken their leave of her parents. 'I have to change.'

'No, of course not,' Rachel answered confidently enough, a wild fluttering sensation beginning in the pit of her stomach. 'Go to his apartment,' he said, so casually, when she had never even known a man who had his own apartment! All the boys she had been out with had lived either with their parents or two or three flatmates, although not for anything would she let Nick St Clare see how nervous the prospect of going to his apartment made her.

'Help yourself to a drink,' he invited once they were inside the luxurious apartment he called home while in England. In Wimbledon itself, conveniently near to the tennis courts, it was the top floor of a two-storey apartment building. 'I'm just going through to shower.'

She ignored the extensive array of drinks, moving nervously about the room, a room only made personal by the magazines lying on the table, the books on the shelf in the Welsh dresser. Her parents' home was comfortable, homely, but this apartment was something else, like one of the pictures in glossy magazines she often drooled over.

'Like it?'

She turned at the sound of Nick's voice, swallowing her shock as she saw he was dressed only in a black silk robe, the smoothness of the material telling her he wore nothing beneath.

She cleared her throat. 'I—er—it's lovely.' She lowered her eyes to the carpet, the memory of his bare legs beneath the robe staying with her. He was more adequately dressed than he was on the tennis court, was more covered at least, and yet the intimacy of this situation unnerved her.

Nick seemed to feel none of her embarrassment, as he came over to drape his arm lightly about her shoulders. 'Do you like Italian food?'

'Er—yes.' Her gaze wouldn't be raised above the open neckline of his robe, the darkly tanned chest, and dark blond hair that grew there.

'Good,' he kissed her lightly, 'because I've booked a table for us at this little Italian restaurant I know.'

'That—that will be nice.' Her mouth actually tingled from that kiss! What was it about this man, and only this man, that made her feel this way?

'I hope so,' he nodded. 'Will you get my clothes out for me while I shower?'

Now she did raise her eyes, stormy grey meeting a more calm blue. 'Get your clothes out?' she gulped.

'Mm, the cream suit and black shirt should do it. Okay?'

'I—Okay,' she nodded agreement, never having performed such an intimate task for a man before.

Nick went into the adjoining bathroom while she sorted through his vast wardrobe for the cream suit and black shirt, the sound of the shower water being turned off just as she found them both.

'O.K.?' Nick came through from the bathroom towelling his hair dry, a darker shade of blond now in its dampness, a towel draped about his waist, his torso completely bare.

Rachel just stared at him. He was like a bronzed god out of Greek mythology, his chest powerfully muscled, as were his legs. His hair was almost dry now, ruffled into disorder, almost returned to its former gold colour.

'Rachel?' he frowned at her silence.

'Er—yes, here you are,' and she thrust the suit and shirt at him before rushing from the room.

CHAPTER THREE

RACHEL was shaking by the time she reached the lounge, pacing the room in agitated movements. Nick might be used to having women in his bedroom, might even be used to women getting his clothes out for him, but she certainly *wasn't* used to doing such things! He had made the request so naturally, and had thought nothing of appearing in front of her in just a robe or towel.

And she had acted like the scared schoolgirl he had first thought her. He was a sophisticated man, of course he had thought nothing of his near-nakedness!

He didn't seem to realise her embarrassment when he came out of the bedroom a short time later either. 'Let's go, hmm?' he suggested lightly.

She let him guide her out to the car, feeling on safer ground away from his home.

By the time they got to the restaurant she had regained her control, instantly liking the intimate atmosphere, the subdued lighting, the red tablecloths on the small tables set some distance apart from each other to allow for greater privacy.

Several heads turned in Nick's direction as they were seated by the portly owner of this small but first class Italian restaurant, although Nick himself seemed immune to those looks of recognition.

'Ignore them,' he advised at her slightly flustered manner.

It was all right for him to say, but she wasn't used to such attention, especially when she was eating. But the red wine Nick ordered with their meal did a lot to settle her nerves, and soon she was as impervious to those curious looks as he was.

'I'll have to take you straight home tonight, I'm afraid,' he informed her as they lingered over their coffee. 'I'm on court at two tomorrow, and Sam will have my hide if I blow that match because of a late night.'

'Sam?' she questioned interestedly.

'Sam Freeman, my coach.'

Rachel nodded. 'I've heard of him.'

'I wouldn't have got anywhere without him,' Nick told her.

He had a genuine affection for the man, she could tell that. 'Didn't he used to play himself?' she asked.

'Years ago,' Nick grinned. 'More years than he would care to remember, I would think. He won quite a few titles in his time.'

Her eyes widened. 'Then he must have been good.'

'He was. Would you like to come and see the match tomorrow?'

She swallowed hard, taken aback. 'Come and watch you play, you mean?'

Nick nodded. 'Well, I'd be insulted if you came to watch anyone else,' he teased. 'You could sit with Sam and Suzy.'

In that special spectators' box for coaches and family, on view to the media and crowd? No, she couldn't do that. She shook her head, smiling to take the sting out of her refusal. 'I don't think so, thank you.'

Nick's expression was suddenly intent, his hand clasping hers across the table. 'Why not?'

'I have college tomorrow——'

'You can miss it for one day, surely?'

'Not really, we have end of the year exams in a week or so.'

'But I'd like you to be there.' He gave her an encouraging smile. 'You never know, you might become my good luck charm.'

'Are you superstitious?' she teased.

'Grow a beard until the end of the championship like Bjorn, you mean?' He shook his head. 'Not really. Although it always upsets my game if I should happen to damage or break my racket in the middle of a match.'

'I'd like to come and watch you,' she said slowly. 'But I really don't think I can.'

'It will only be for the afternoon, Rachel.'

'I—All right,' she nodded. After all, she could afford to miss one afternoon of college. 'How will I get in?'

'I'll leave word with Sam.' Nick was smiling broadly now that he had his own way.

'And who is Suzy?' she asked casually, not having missed the mention of the other girl.

He laughed softly, seeing through her casualness. 'Why, Rachel, who do you think she is?'

She blushed. 'I have no idea.' And she was jealous! Two days of knowing this man and she was jealous of him even mentioning another girl!

'Suzy is Sam's daughter,' he mocked her. 'And I've known her since she wore braces on her teeth.'

He spoke of her with the affection of an older brother, so Rachel dismissed her from her mind. 'Maybe we should be going now if you have to be alert for the match tomorrow,' she suggested softly.

'Yes,' he sighed. 'Sometimes I wonder if it's worth it.' He signalled for the bill to be brought over.

'Surely when you win——'

'Ah, when you win,' he nodded. 'But when you

lose. . .! Sometimes I'm out on court and I know there isn't a damn thing I can do to win, that on that particular day my opponent is too good to beat, and I may have another two gruelling sets to play before it's all over.'

'It sounds like hard work,' she grimaced.

'Oh, it is,' he gave a rueful smile. 'And tomorrow Paul will make sure I run more miles than I want to.'

'Paul Shepley?' She found it really strange the way he referred to people she had only ever seen on the television by their first names, although from what she had read, although they were highly competitive on court, a lot of the tennis players were good friends off court.

'That's right.' He stood up. 'And I'm afraid we both have tempers, so it should be a volatile match.'

Until Paul Shepley came on the tennis scene Nick had been the bad boy of the game. Rachel had seen both men blow up at what they thought was a wrong call by officials, and of the two she thought Nick the more controlled. Maybe maturity had mellowed him.

Although he didn't appear in the least controlled as he kissed her goodnight, the car parked outside her home, his lips fevered against hers, his hands seeming to burn where they touched.

'I don't want to make a habit of this,' he murmured against her mouth, his eyes stormy.

'Of what?' she asked breathlessly.

'Making love to you in my car,' he smiled. 'It's too confining. And too damned public,' he scowled as a man walking his dog peered in the window at them.

'Would you like to come in for coffee?' Rachel offered to cover her embarrassment.

'Will your parents still be up?'

She looked at her watch. 'Ten-thirty. No, they

should be in bed by now. They usually watch the news and then go up.'

Nick grinned, already opening his car door. 'Then I'd love a cup of coffee!'

He came round to open her door for her, and Rachel absently noted how the street-lamps made his hair look almost silver.

He seemed overpowering once they were inside the house, and he made no effort to pretend he was really interested in coffee, sweeping her into his arms, her body curved into his as his mouth tasted hers, biting enticingly on her bottom lip before his mouth strayed across her cheek and down to her throat.

'Rachel,' he groaned. 'Rachel, I——'

'Is that you, dear?' The lounge light was suddenly switched on and her embarrassed mother stood in the doorway in her dressing-gown, her hair in rollers, her face bare of make-up. 'Oh, I—I'm so sorry,' she said in a flustered voice. 'I didn't realise you had Mr St Clare with you, Rachel.'

Nick moved away from Rachel with an assurance she could only admire, smoothing his golden hair. 'Please excuse us, Mrs James. After all, it's your lounge.'

'Yes, but I—Don't be long, dear. Goodnight, Mr St Clare,' and her mother made a hasty exit.

'Whoops!' Nick chuckled. 'You don't usually make love with your men friends in your parents' home, I take it?'

'No,' Rachel choked, as embarrassed as her mother had been.

'And you would rather she hadn't seen us together this time?' His hands were linked loosely about her waist as he looked down at her.

'Yes,' she admitted miserably.

'I'll go now, and you can go upstairs and explain to

her that it was just a harmless kiss.' He released her. 'The next time I make love to you I'll make sure we aren't going to be interrupted.'

The next time . . .?

'I'll look out for you tomorrow.' He gently touched her cheek.

'Good luck,' Rachel said shyly.

He grimaced. 'I have an idea I'm going to need it.'

Her mother and father were reading in bed when she got upstairs, her hair combed back into neatness after Nick had run his fingers through it.

'I'm so sorry, Rachel,' her mother put her book down. 'I just didn't realise . . .'

'That's all right, Mum,' she blushed.

'Have a nice evening, dear?' her father asked vaguely.

'Er—very nice.' She shot a questioning look at her mother, who gently shook her head. At least her father didn't know of the embarrassing scene her mother had interrupted! 'Mr St Clare has invited me to watch him play tomorrow,' she told them excitedly, her embarrassment forgotten in her pleasure.

Her mother frowned. 'But surely that's in the afternoon?'

'It won't hurt to miss one afternoon of college, Mum. I may never get another chance like this,' Rachel added pleadingly.

'I suppose not, dear . . .'

'He'll be leaving town again soon,' she pushed home her point, 'so I don't have many more chances to see him. Oh, do say yes, Mum!'

'All right, Rachel,' her mother nodded after several minutes. 'Maybe I'll even see you on television, hmm?' she teased gently, to ease Rachel's tension.

'Maybe,' Rachel nodded eagerly.

She hardly slept because she was so excited. She was actually going to be Nick St Clare's personal guest, was going to sit with his coach. Everyone would realise why she was there. Oh, she had never felt so nervous in her life before!

Hilary was very contrite for her gossiping the next day, although she spoilt her apology by adding. 'But it taught Danny a lesson.' She smiled her pleasure. 'You should have seen his face when you drove off with Nick St Clare!'

'You should have seen mine!' Rachel giggled.

'I did,' Hilary laughed. 'I must have been mad to have refused the lift when it was offered,' she groaned.

'I knew you'd regret it.'

'The moment I said it!'

'That's what I thought,' Rachel nodded.

'And now you're actually going to watch him play,' Hilary said enviously.

Rachel looked at her watch. 'And I'd better get going, otherwise I'll be late.'

'Danny's going to be *green* when he hears about this,' her friend said with glee.

Rachel raised her eyebrows. 'He isn't going to hear about it—is he?' she warned.

'Not from me,' Hilary feigned innocence. 'He could just see you on television, you know.'

'Oh lord, yes,' she groaned. 'I hope not.'

'I hope so,' Hilary protested. 'I'm going home right now and switch on the television on the basis of that.'

'But what about your classes?'

'What about yours?' Hilary returned cheekily.

Indeed, what about hers? She didn't even give them a second thought as she made her way to Wimbledon. Today she was wearing black fitted trousers and a white high-necked silk blouse, her long hair clean and shiny. Nick wasn't going to be ashamed of the way she looked.

Wimbledon was a hive of activity, people milling everywhere, and as she stood at the gate she felt sure Nick must have forgotten all about inviting her. He would have so much else on his mind today, he could easily have forgotten.

'Miss James?'

She turned eagerly at the sound of that brittle female voice. Nick had remembered after all, had sent someone to meet her.

But the woman in front of her wasn't what she had been expecting; she was a tall slender blonde of about twenty-five, with one of the most beautiful faces Rachel had ever seen. Deep blue eyes, a short straight nose, a plum-coloured lip-gloss emphasising the perfection of her pouting mouth, hair almost the same gold as Nick's, waving loosely to her shoulders, the brown dress she wore drawing attention to the fullness of her breasts, the slimness of her waist, her gently curving thighs and long slender legs, had to make her one of the sexiest-looking women Rachel had ever seen too.

The woman looked like a fashion model, and whoever she was Rachel felt sure there had been some sort of mistake. Nick couldn't possibly have asked this woman to meet her.

'Miss James?' she repeated irritably as Rachel continued to stare at her.

'I—er—Yes,' she answered dazedly. 'But I don't think——'

The woman was looking her over speculatively, obviously not listening to her. 'I must say you aren't quite what I'd been expecting,' she drawled.

'I'm not?' She swallowed hard, clutching her handbag to her.

'No,' the girl's mouth twisted. 'When Nick told me he'd promised one of his little fans a ringside seat, and that you needed to be met, I naturally assumed you would be—younger, more of a child.'

She had made an enemy of this woman, and she didn't even know why! 'Maybe that's how Nick thinks of me,' she said dully, wondering if that could be true.

'I'm sure it is,' the other girl nodded coolly. 'He said he owed you a favour for helping his sister out.'

Why did the afternoon suddenly look so gloomy— even though it was bright sunshine! For once Wimbledon had remained mainly rain-free, most of the matches being played on time. 'Yes,' she acknowledged dully.

'We'd better get going.' The girl looked impatiently at her slender gold wrist-watch. 'The match will be starting in a moment. I'm Suzy Freeman, by the way,' and she turned and began walking quickly in the direction of Centre Court.

Rachel followed—mainly because she knew it was expected of her. *This* was Suzy Freeman, Nick's coach's daughter, the girl Nick had dismissed as if *she* were no more than a schoolgirl. Maybe that was how he thought of both of them?

She looked at the way Suzy Freeman walked, deliberately swinging her hips, and knew that no man could think of her as a child, not even a man who had known her since she 'wore braces on her teeth'.

The players were already on court warming up when she and Suzy Freeman took their seats, although Sam Freeman leant forward in his seat and said a few words of welcome to her, obviously tense as he waited for the match to begin.

Rachel had first taken a serious interest in tennis

about two years ago, when she had been off school at the time of Wimbledon with 'flu, watching the tennis on television because she felt too awful to do anything else. By the time she went back to school 'flu wasn't the only bug she had caught. She had even taken up tennis herself after that, and could put in quite a good amateur game.

But the two men on court were anything but amateurs, both strong players, and both determined to win. It looked like being a tough match, for both men, and the air on the Centre Court seemed to crackle with the tension of it.

Nick was totally immersed in the game ahead, looking to neither left nor right as he concentrated on practising his serve. A hush fell over the court as they were signalled to begin playing.

For the next three hours Rachel sat on the edge of her seat, each point fought over, each game fought for, until at the end of two hours each player had two sets, the fifth and deciding set going to a tie-breaker—which Paul Shepley won!

Tears came into her eyes as she saw the look of disappointment on Nick's face as he lost that last vital point, although it was quickly masked as he moved forward to congratulate his opponent.

'Oh dear,' Suzy sighed as her father pushed past them on his way to meet Nick. 'Now the fun's going to start!'

'Surely it's over?' Rachel said dejectedly, disappointed on Nick's behalf. He had played so well, so calmly for him, and he should have won. But it was no good saying that, he hadn't won, and he must be feeling awful at this moment.

'Oh no,' Suzy's mouth twisted as the two of them filed out. 'Now comes the post-mortem on why Nick lost.'

'But he could so easily have won——'

'Yes, which is why my father will want to know why he didn't. Believe me, they'll spend hours going over what was done and what should have been done.'

'Nick did all he could,' Rachel defended.

'But he didn't win. And Dad will want to know why.'

Rachel looked down at her hands. 'Does that mean I won't be able to see Nick?' she asked quietly.

'Did he say you would?' Suzy raised her eyebrows.

'Well . . . no. But I—I assumed——'

The other girl shrugged. 'Nick gave me the impression he'd just asked you to the match, he made no mention of seeing you later.'

Rachel looked frustratedly at Suzy Freeman. Nick *hadn't* mentioned seeing her after the match, so maybe he hadn't intended to. Could it possibly be that she had thrown his gratitude for helping his sister out of all proportion?

'Besides,' Suzy added throatily, 'Nick and I usually go out alone after a match, either to console or congratulate him.' She looked Rachel over scathingly. 'I doubt you could—console him, in the same way.'

Colour flooded Rachel's cheeks as the implication of the other girl's words hit her. Nick and Suzy . . .? But why not, Suzy was more his age, more than shared his interest in tennis. And she was beautiful.

'Thank you for looking after me this afternoon, Miss Freeman——'

'Suzy, please,' she invited graciously.

'Suzy,' Rachel said jerkily. 'I've appreciated it,' she fidgeted nervously with the strap of her handbag. 'Er— I'll go now.'

'I'm glad you've enjoyed yourself.' The other girl

was all sweetness now. 'I'm sorry Nick didn't win.'

'So am I. Tell him that, will you?'

'Of course,' Suzy smiled. 'Well, I'd better go and save Nick from my father. He can be a bit of a bear when he loses.'

'Nick or your father?'

'Both,' Suzy laughed huskily. 'I usually act as referee.'

'Then I won't keep you,' Rachel told her brittlely. 'Goodbye.'

'Goodbye, Rachel. And I'll give Nick your condolences.'

'Thank you.' She turned and walked away, hoping against hope that she would make it to the exit before she began crying.

She was soon swallowed up in the rest of the crowd leaving the grounds, almost running by the time she got outside.

But what had she expected? Nick's invitation to watch him play had been casually given, and although she might not have accepted it in the same way he wasn't to know that.

'You're home early, love,' her mother said in surprise as Rachel let herself into the house. 'I somehow didn't expect you home for dinner.' She added an extra chop to the grill.

Rachel put her handbag down on a worktop. 'You saw the match?'

'Yes,' her mother said sympathetically. 'I don't suppose Mr St Clare felt much like company after that.'

It depended what sort of 'company' it was! 'No,' Rachel agreed dully.

'Dinner's nearly ready,' her mother turned the chops over. 'I should go and get washed.'

'Yes, Mum.' Rachel went obediently up the stairs,

not really having an appetite for dinner but knowing her mother wouldn't understand if she refused it.

'I've knitted this matinee coat for Mrs Lennox's little girl,' her mother told her after the meal, holding up the pretty pink woollen garment. 'Do you think she'll like it?'

'Oh, Mum, it's beautiful!' Rachel took the delicate article of clothing into her own hands, marvelling at its perfection. 'It's really lovely,' she added softly. 'But when did you knit it?'

'I started it last night and finished it off while I watched the tennis today.' Her mother was flushed with pleasure. 'It doesn't take long to make something as small as that.'

'Small as it is, I still think it will be a little on the large side for Eve Rachel. Did I tell you that was the name they had decided on?' Rachel had been thrilled that the baby's second name was to be her own.

'I think I saw it on the card Mr Lennox sent with the flowers,' her mother nodded. 'We saw you on television this afternoon, by the way.'

Rachel's eyes widened. 'You did?' She hadn't been aware of a television camera being on her.

'Mm,' her mother nodded excitedly. 'A couple of times the camera went to Mr St Clare's coach, and you were sitting quite close to him, weren't you?'

'Mm,' she nodded, still touching the softness of the little pink jacket.

'Who was the girl sitting between you?' her mother asked casually.

Rachel concentrated on putting the cardigan back in its paper bag. 'Oh, that was Mr Freeman's daughter Suzy.'

'Mr St Clare's coach?'

'Yes,' she nodded, deliberately not looking at her mother.

'She's very pretty.'

'Yes. Do you think it's too late to take this jacket to the hospital now?' Rachel changed the subject, not wanting to remember how beautiful Suzy Freeman was.

Her mother frowned. 'I'm sure it isn't. But——'

'Then I think I'll take it over,' she stood up decisively. 'I shouldn't be long.'

'But, Rachel——'

'Yes?' She turned at the door.

'Nothing,' her mother shrugged. 'Don't be late, dear, you have college tomorrow.'

It didn't take long to reach the hospital, and the bus she travelled on was almost empty, most of the windows open in the heat of the evening. A young girl on the reception desk directed her to Kay Lennox's room, and she knocked tentatively on the door. To her surprise the door was opened by a rather serious-looking man of about thirty, his dark hair short, his three-piece suit very formal.

'Rachel!' Key Lennox cried her recognition. 'Don't keep Rachel standing at the door, Richard,' she told the man impatiently.

Richard Lennox wasn't at all what she had been expecting; he looked rather serious compared to his wife's bubbly personality. But then they said opposites attracted, and in this case it seemed to be true.

'Thank your mother so much for me,' Kay said warmly when she had unwrapped the matinee coat and the introductions had been made.

'I thought it might be a little big,' she frowned.

'The way that young lady is eating she'll soon grow into it!' Richard Lennox showed that his serious nature hid a lighter side.

'Here, have a cuddle,' Kay thrust the baby at her.

Rachel took the tiny bundle nervously into her arms, finding a pair of huge blue eyes looking vaguely up at her; the baby was too young to focus yet.

'She won't break,' Kay grinned. 'I treated her like porcelain the first day, was almost afraid of her——'

'And now she throws her about like she's a sack of coal,' added a mocking voice.

'Nick!' Kay cried excitedly.

Rachel turned in time to see him coming fully inside the room and closing the door behind him, his denims and shirt very casual, lines of weariness about his eyes and mouth.

'Rachel,' he nodded to her distantly.

She swallowed hard. 'Nick.' Her voice was husky.

'What happened to you this afternoon?' Kay tactlessly asked her brother. 'I really thought you had him.'

'So did I,' Nick grimaced, no longer looking at Rachel—in fact, he was ignoring her. 'But I had a few minutes' lack of concentration and—well, he took advantage of it.'

'Maybe next year,' Richard encouraged.

Nick shrugged. 'I doubt there will be a next year.'

'You aren't talking about retirement again?' his sister scorned.

Rachel was aware of being in on an intimate fammily discussion, and she walked over to the window, staring out at the busy road at the side of the hospital. Although she tried not to listen, talking softly to the baby, she could still hear the conversation going on behind her.

'I can't go on playing for ever,' Nick was saying now.

'But you don't have to retire at thirty either!' Kay derided.

'I have enough money——'

'I'm not talking about the money,' his sister dismissed. 'Although goodness knows you have enough of it.'

'He's earnt it, Kay,' Richard put in quietly.

'I'm not disputing that,' his wife nodded. 'But thirty isn't old. Look at Newcombe——'

'I'm not in his class,' Nick drawled.

'Don't talk rubbish,' Kay snapped. 'Good grief, Nick, you lost one match——'

'And it lost me my chance in the final.'

'There's no shame in losing to Paul Shepley!'

'I didn't say there was,' he sighed. 'I just think maybe it's time I dropped out.'

'When you can still get to a semi-final of Wimbledon it isn't time to retire yet,' Kay protested.

Rachel had to agree with her, shocked by the suggestion that Nick might give up playing professional tennis. But it wasn't for her to make any comment. Not that she thought Nick would listen to her opinion anyway!

He was in a very down mood, totally unlike the teasing man she had spent the evening with yesterday, and she wondered what had happened to Suzy Freeman's efforts to 'console' him. Maybe she hadn't started yet—after all, it was still early, they could be meeting later.

'What do you think, Rachel?' Kay's question interrupted her disturbing thoughts.

She turned with a start. 'Sorry?' she blinked her puzzlement.

'Don't you think Nick's too good to retire yet?' Kay asked her.

She glanced nervously at Nick but could tell nothing of his thoughts from his enigmatic expression. 'I'm sure Mr St Clare isn't interested in my opinion,' she said stiltedly.

'On the contrary,' he drawled, 'I would be very interested.'

She shrugged, evading the mockery in his eyes. 'I agree with your sister,' she said coolly. 'When you can still reach a Wimbledon semi-final then you're still far from the retirement stage.'

'Really?' he taunted.

Her eyes flashed. 'Yes, really!'

'You see?' Kay said knowingly, immune to the strained atmosphere between her brother and Rachel.

Rachel was wondering at that strain herself. What had she done that almost seemed to have angered Nick? It wasn't just his disappointment at losing the match, it was a veiled anger, a veiled anger directed at her. And she had no idea why!

'See what?' he asked his sister.

'You're still good, Nick,' she sighed.

'Not good enough.' His tone was grim.

'You're just on a downer,' she told him. 'Once you get to Boston and start your next tournament you'll feel a hundred per cent better.'

His mouth twisted. 'Believe me, the way I feel right now, that still wouldn't be too good.'

'Oh, Nick, snap out of it,' Kay dismissed impatiently. 'Some uncle you are—you haven't even looked at Eve!'

'That's because Rachel had been monopolising her ever since I came in.'

Hot colour flooded Rachel's cheeks, and she thrust the baby into his arms. 'Sorry,' she muttered. 'Excuse me,' and she hurried from the room, blinking back the tears.

It was too much—too much on top of Suzy

Freeman's patronising dismissal of her this afternoon. Nick really had invited her to the match out of gratitude, had even taken his 'little fan' out to dinner last night as an added bonus, only she had seen more into it than there really was, had been so starry-eyed she hadn't wanted to see the truth.

'Rachel?'

She turned sharply and came face to face with Nick. 'Mr St Clare,' she said stiffly.

His brows rose. 'Mr St Clare?' he queried softly.

Her head went back. 'It's your name.'

'A few minutes ago it was Nick.'

A few minutes ago she hadn't realised he thought of her as a child. 'Sorry,' she muttered again.

His mouth tightened perceptibly. 'Are you?'

Rachel shrugged with feigned nonchalance. 'If you would rather I call you Nick then I will. For the brief time we shall be in conversation it will be no hardship.'

'Rachel . . .?'

'Yes—Nick?' her voice was stilted.

'Why are you so damned mad when you're the one who walked out on me?' he rasped, mockery forgotten in his anger.

'Oh, I didn't!' she gasped.

'You left,' he stated flatly.

'Yes, but—Wasn't I supposed to?' she asked hesitantly.

'You know damn well I wanted to spend the night with you, whether I won or lost.'

She thought he had, until Suzy Freeman had told her differently. But what of Suzy Freeman now? Nick certainly wasn't with her, and he didn't sound as if he intended to be either.

'Miss Freeman—Suzy——'

'Passed on your message,' he said grimly.

Rachel frowned. 'What message?'

His mouth twisted bitterly. 'The one about how sorry you were that I'd lost—and goodbye.'

'Good—goodbye?'

'Yes!' He thrust his hands into his denims pocket. 'No one loves a loser, do they, Rachel?' he scorned.

She froze. 'What do you mean?'

Nick shrugged. 'It's obvious—I lost, you left. It can't be any clearer than that.'

He thought—he really thought——! 'It can be clearer to me!' she told him angrily. 'I didn't leave because you lost, I left because—because——'

'Yes?' he taunted sceptically.

She couldn't betray Suzy Freeman's part in this. Besides, she had no idea if the other girl had really meant to deceive her, and Suzy had known Nick a lot longer than she had, so Nick might not believe her even if she did tell him the truth.

'I thought you would rather be alone,' she evaded.

'When I'd just lost one of the most important matches of my career!' he derided. 'I wanted to spend the night with you!'

Rachel flushed. 'Miss Freeman gave me the impression——'

'Don't bring Suzy into this,' he rasped. 'You involved her enough just by asking her to say goodbye to me. Couldn't you at least have——'

'I didn't say goodbye to you!' she insisted fiercely.

'Didn't you?'

'No!' She glared at him. 'I just thought you wanted to be alone. And that's the truth,' she added as he went to speak.

Nick gave her a considering look. 'Prove it,' he finally challenged.

'P-prove it?'

'Have dinner with me,' he prompted softly.

She searched his face for some sign of mockery—and found none. He really did think she didn't want to be with him! 'I've already eaten,' she refused dazedly.

'A drink, then?' he pounced.

'I—Yes, a—a drink would be lovely,' she accepted eagerly.

'Wait here for me,' he instructed curtly. 'I'd better go and reassure my sister that we're friends again. After the way you rushed out she seems to think I must have upset you in some way.'

Rachel stood patiently in the corridor while Nick took his leave of his sister and brother-in-law. He seemed to think he was actually forcing her to spend the rest of the evening with him, seemed to have no idea that she could imagine nothing she would rather do.

'Ready?' his appearance back at her side interrupted her thoughts.

'Yes,' she nodded coolly, wondering if Nick would be quite so attentive if he knew how eager she was. The indulgent amusement of yesterday had gone now, and the light of desire burning in his deep blue eyes held more than a passing interest.

He opened the car door for her, turning to grin at her as he got in beside her. 'I feel like getting drunk, like to join me?'

'I——'

'I forgot, you don't like to drink,' he grimaced. 'Right now I need a drink, and I feel like having company.' He put the car into gear and moved out into the road.

'I didn't say I don't like to drink,' hot colour burned her cheeks. 'I had some wine last night. I just didn't drink a lot because I had college today,' she defended.

'So you'll join me tonight?'

She had college again tomorrow, but not for anything would she use that as an excuse. 'Yes,' she agreed stiltedly.

'Talking of college, did your boy-friend have anything to say to you today?' Nick sounded amused.

Danny had had quite a lot to say, and most of it had been insulting. Rachel had finally walked out of the canteen, leaving her coffee untouched, his nasty comments still following her.

But she wasn't going to tell Nick of Danny's juvenile behaviour. She wished she had never been involved with the younger man, and his behaviour now sickened her. 'No,' she lied.

'No?' Nick quirked a disbelieving eyebrow.

'No,' she insisted stubbornly, looking about her interestedly. 'Where are we going?'

'I said I wanted to get drunk,' he repeated grimly. 'I don't need a drunken driving charge added to my misery.'

Rachel gave him a startled look. 'Meaning . . .?'

'Meaning we're going to my apartment for that drink.'

She remembered all too vividly the embarrassment she had suffered when they had gone to his home last night. And the reckless mood he was in tonight didn't seem to point to his behaving any more discreetly.

CHAPTER FOUR

SHE was a bundle of nerves by the time they entered Nick's apartment a few minutes later, unsure of his mood and yet unwilling to act childishly again by asking to be taken home.

Nick moved straight to the drinks cupboard, pouring himself a liberal amount of whisky. 'Want one?' he held up the glass.

Rachel's hands twisted nervously together in front of her. 'Er—Do you have any wine?'

'Wine?' he repeated slowly, disbelievingly.

Hot colour flooded her cheeks. 'Yes, wine. White, actually,' she added in a challenging tone.

His expression left her in no doubt as to his disgust at such a request. 'I guess so,' he answered finally. 'On the wine rack in the kitchen. I'll go and get some. Sweet or dry?'

'Dry, please. And preferably sparkling.'

His eyebrows rose even further. 'Are you sure you wouldn't like champagne? To toast the loser?'

His bitterness made her bite her lips painfully. 'No champagne,' she answered coolly—in fact, later she was sure she would be amazed at the confidence she had displayed. 'Just a sparkling wine. Asti Spumante, or something like that.'

'I'll see what I've got,' Nick muttered.

Rachel breathed a sigh of relief when he at last disappeared into the kitchen, feeling as if she had been with a time-bomb the last half an hour—and it could explode at any moment!

'Here you go,' Nick came back with a bottle of wine. 'Asti Spumante, as requested.' He poured some into two glasses, taking a large swallow from one of them. 'Mm, not bad,' he refilled the glass, carrying the other one over to Rachel. 'Madam,' he handed it to her with a flourish.

She accepted the drink, eyeing him warily. She wasn't sure she liked him in this mood of sarcasm bordering on cruelty, and she didn't like the way he was mixing his drinks, his reckless mood seeming to increase by the minute.

His anger and disappointment at losing this afternoon seemed all the more surprising because of his calmness and good sportsmanship once the match had been over. Then he had seemed to accept his defeat with good grace; now his bitterness had taken over.

'Like some more?' he held out the bottle, refilling his own glass.

'No, thank you. I—Do you think you should?' she asked nervously.

Nick gave her a wolfish grin. 'Should what?'

Her cheeks coloured bright red. 'Drink so much,' she said waspishly. 'You'll only have a headache tomorrow.'

'Maybe.' He lounged down on the sofa, his feet up on the coffee table, the bottle of wine discarded in favour of the whisky bottle. 'But tonight, with you, I'm going to feel bloody fantastic.'

Rachel stood up. 'Maybe I should go——'

'Sit down,' he ordered roughly.

'I—I beg your pardon?'

He sighed, running a weary hand over his eyes. 'Sorry,' he muttered. 'I'm afraid I'm forgetting the social graces tonight.'

'Then you would rather be alone——'

'No!' his denial was harsh. 'For God's sake, Rachel, stop talking about leaving. I need you tonight. I need your beauty, your youth. Stay with me, Rachel!' His eyes were pleading.

She subsided back into her seat, unwilling to leave him if he really did need her. 'Your sister seems very happy,' she attempted conversation.

'There isn't much gets Kay down.'

'Oh, I'm sorry. I didn't mean——'

'I know you didn't.' Nick swallowed some more of his whisky. 'Kay is one of those people who's always happy. Richard is the opposite, a pessimist.'

'I gathered.'

Nick nodded. 'Somehow, between them, they have one of the happiest marriages I've ever seen. Richard brings Kay down to earth, and Kay gets him out of his blacker moods.'

'They live here in London?' Somehow it was easier talking about other people, less explosive.

He shrugged. 'Richard is a Londoner, and Kay doesn't mind where she lives as long as she's with him.'

'That's nice.'

'Like I said, they have a happy marriage.'

The rapidity with which Nick refilled his glass with whisky worried Rachel over the next couple of hours, especially as his voice seemed to be becoming more and more slurred as the evening progressed. But other than that slight slurring of his words he remained otherwise lucid, his conversation witty, his expression alert.

To her dismay Rachel saw he had almost drunk the whole contents of a bottle of whisky, while she was still on her second glass of wine. He certainly wasn't in any condition to drive her home.

Suddenly he swayed to his feet. 'Help me to bed, will you?'

At last he seemed to be acting sensibly! 'Of course.' She was instantly at his side, her arm about his waist, his about her shoulders as she helped him into the bedroom she had entered only once before.

Nick sat down heavily on the bed. 'You'll have to help me undress,' he began to unbutton his shirt.

Rachel licked her lips nervously. 'Couldn't you just—keep your clothes on?'

His mouth twisted derisvely. 'Hardly.'

She felt as if she had eight thumbs and only two fingers as she helped him off with his shirt; the tee-shirts he wore on court only hinted at his muscled back and shoulders, his skin tanned a golden brown. She faltered as his hands moved to the belt and fastening of his denims, although she seemed to have little choice but to remove those too when Nick suddenly collapsed back against the pillow. The white shorts he wore on court were brief enough, but the black underpants he wore beneath his denims barely covered him, his legs long and muscular, the dark blond hair on his chest continuing over his navel and lower, disappearing beneath the waistband of his underpants.

Rachel decided to leave this last article of clothing, pulling the covers up over his unconscious form. As she moved to the bedroom door the telephone began ringing in the lounge, and she made a hurried dash to answer it before its loud noise woke Nick up.

'Yes?' she said breathlessly into the receiver.

'Who is that?' demanded a familiar female voice.

Suzy Freeman! And she sounded as if she had a right to object to Nick having another woman in his apartment. 'It's Rachel James,' she told her.

'Rachel——! Can I talk to Nick?' The other girl's

voice had hardened to anger.

'Er—Not at the moment,' Rachel answered evasively. After all, he might not want his coach's daughter knowing he was blind drunk, no matter what his own relationship with Suzy was.

'Why not?' Suzy snapped.

'I—He's asleep. He—He was tired.'

'Oh yes?' The other girl sounded sceptical.

'Yes. You see, he——'

'Who's that on the phone?' drawled a blurred voice from behind her.

Rachel turned with a start, hastily turning away again as she saw Nick was still wearing only the brief black underpants, not having bothered to pull on a robe or anything to cover him. His blond hair was ruffled, his blue eyes slightly unfocused, and if it weren't for the unmistakable maturity of his bronzed body he would have looked like a little boy just roused from sleep.

She held the receiver out to him. 'It's Miss Freeman,' she mumbled.

A frown marred his brow. 'What the hell does she want?'

'I have no idea. But I think you should talk to her.'

'Okay.' He took the receiver, grasping Rachel's wrist in the other hand as she would have moved away. 'Don't go,' he requested huskily.

'Oh, but——'

'Stay, Rachel.' His fingers tightened about her wrist.

'All right,' she averted her eyes, looking anywhere but at Nick, but conscious of him all the same, of the sensuality he exuded, the fundamental male smell that she couldn't ignore when standing this close to him.

'Hi, Suzy,' he spoke into the receiver. 'Mind your

own damned business!' he rasped. 'Get off my back, Suzy,' he added in a weary voice. 'When I want your advice I'll damn well ask for it!' He slammed the receiver down, glaring at it in his anger.

Rachel licked her lips nervously, still not able to look at him. 'What did she want?'

'To tell me how to run my life,' he scowled. 'And nobody does that.'

'No?'

'No! Hey,' his voice softened as he turned to face her, 'why are we arguing?'

'I—You——'

He pulled her up against his nakedness. 'You shouldn't have let me fall asleep,' he chided gently.

Rachel flushed. 'As I remember it I didn't *let* you do anything. And I don't think you were sleeping, you'd passed out.'

Nick shook his head. 'If I had passed out I'd still be that way. This afternoon's match and the whisky made me fall asleep. But I'm awake now,' he added softly. 'Maybe I have something to thank Suzy for after all.'

'You do?'

'Mm,' he nodded. 'You were just about to sneak out of here, weren't you?'

Rachel wished he wouldn't hold her quite so close, wished she couldn't feel every hard contour of his body. 'I was about to leave, yes.' She held herself away from him as much as she could with her hands on his chest, his skin firm and warm beneath her touch.

'And if Suzy's telephone call hadn't woken me I would have woken up alone.'

She flushed. 'You'll be doing that anyway.' She began to push against him in earnest, finding his arms had suddenly tightened about her waist, feeling like steel bands.

'Hey, look, I'm sorry about the way I've behaved tonight,' his voice was huskily persuasive. 'But I'm over it now, both the anger and the booze.'

And strangely he was. Those few minutes' sleep seemed to have restored him to his usual charming self, the slurredness was gone from his voice, the bitterness from his manner.

'I have to go, Nick——'

'Of course you don't,' he soothed. 'I just told you, I'm all right now.'

'Yes, but——'

'I'm all right, Rachel.' His hands moved to cup either side of her face as he bent his head to kiss her lingeringly on the mouth. 'You have such lovely lips, Rachel,' he murmured throatily. 'Soft and inviting, with a taste of——'

'They taste of wine,' she mocked to hide her embarrassment.

Nick gave a throaty chuckle. 'I was going to say honey, but as you must consider me something of an alcoholic after tonight I don't think I'd better liken wine to honey. I need a shower, Rachel, and then I'll be fine. Okay?'

'Maybe I should just go——'

'No,' he insisted forcibly. 'I still need you. I don't want to be alone tonight.'

'All right,' she sighed. She could hardly leave him when he said he needed her!

'Five minutes,' he promised, kissing her lightly on the nose.

Rachel wandered aimlessly into the lounge once he had gone. She would have to leave soon, it was almost eleven o'clock, and her parents had no idea where she was, although they might have guessed she was with Nick.

'Rachel . . .'

She turned at the husky sound of his voice, finding him freshly showered, his hair still damp, a towel wrapped about his waist.

He came slowly towards her. 'I should have asked you if you would like a shower too,' he said softly.

'Er—no, I don't think so.'

'Rachel!' His mouth moved sensually against her throat, the hardness of his thighs erotic against hers. 'Oh Rachel, I want you!' he groaned, his mouth taking possession of hers.

The heated passion of his words and mouth caused her to melt against him, returning the kiss as her body arched against his, each muscle and sinew moulded against her, the drugging movement of his mouth on hers causing a liquid fire in her veins.

As he lifted her in his arms and carried her through to the bedrooms she knew only pleasure, helping him with the buttons of her blouse as he laid her gently on the bed, arching her breasts up to meet the warm possession of his mouth, shuddering as she felt the heated lick of his tongue against her taut nipple, one of his hands coming up to clasp the other breast as his mouth moved to claim it.

There was a slow warmth spreading through her limbs, a burning ache in her body that she had never known before. But no man had ever touched her in this way before, her nipples aching from his touch, her skin seeming to burn as Nick caressed her waist and thighs with his hands.

She felt the warm air on her naked skin as Nick released the fastening on her trousers, raised her body as he smoothed the material down her thighs, her protest as he also discarded her bikini briefs swallowed up in his kiss, his lips exploring her mouth introducing further intimacy. And all the time he was caressing her breasts, teasing and tormenting the nipples until she groaned her dissatisfaction, sighing her pleasure as his mouth once again possessed a throbbing peak.

She was lost in such a world of sensual pleasure, of shuddering ecstasy, that when Nick's body possessed hers completely she felt only a brief stabbing pain before she was engulfed in such wild sensations she never wanted the moment to end, wanted to remain one with Nick in this way for ever.

Nick lost control after her initial groan of pain, was taking her with a fierceness that carried them both to the highest peak, bearing Rachel over the edge with him as pleasure filled every particle of her body, her flesh completely in accord with Nick's as the ecstasy went on and on into oblivion.

It did seem almost as if she had passed out for a moment, but she knew she must only have slept, the complete satiation of her body causing her to fall into an exhausted sleep.

She opened her eyes to find Nick dressed and sitting in the bedroom chair, the smile fading from her lips and eyes as he looked down at her broodingly. His expression frightened her, there was none of the warmth of a lover in his icy blue eyes.

'Just what did you hope to achieve?' he rasped suddenly.

Rachel was suddenly conscious of how she must look spreadeagled on the bed, and hastily pulled on her blouse, warm colour in her cheeks as Nick clinically watched her pull on her briefs and trousers. She felt awful with him looking at her so coldly, almost as if he hated her. Perhaps he did, she thought hysterically. What must he think of her, allowing him to make love to her when she had only known him three days!

What did she think of herself! She hardly knew Nick St Clare, except to know he was a brilliant tennis player who hated to lose, and that he liked and appreciated women. And that he had a lot of experience at making love! He had known exactly what to do to reduce her to a pliant, lovesick—*love*sick? Where did *love* come into this? Surely she didn't love Nick St Clare?

Her parents had the sort of love she had always wanted, the sort of love you grew into, and which grew with you. You couldn't love a person you didn't know, not really love them. Maybe physical attraction——

'I asked you a question, damn you!' Nick harshly interrupted her wandering thoughts.

Rachel licked her lips nervously, sitting on the bed, her legs feeling as if they were made of cotton-wool. 'I don't know what you mean,' she told him raggedly, wondering if this angry stranger could really have whispered those erotic things in her ear as their bodies joined together.

'You know,' he sighed, standing up to agitatedly pace the room, the last signs of the alcohol he had consumed completely gone now, 'I don't know why I didn't think of it before. I thought you were like the other women I've met, that you knew the score, and instead you're a *virgin*! Just tell me one thing,' his mouth twisted. 'Was your meeting with Kay as accidental as it seemed to be, or did you engineer it to meet me?'

'I could hardly arrange your sister's pregnancy,' she flashed.

'Only your own, it would seem,' Nick muttered, his mouth white with anger.

Rachel paled, her hands suddenly feeling clammy. 'I—What do you mean?'

'Don't try to act as if you just came out of a convent,'

he scorned. 'You know what I mean as well as I do!'

'I—I don't know what you're talking about. If you want me to leave then just say so, there's no need to be unpleasant——'

'Unpleasant! How bloody English!' he taunted. 'Let me tell you, I haven't even *started* to get unpleasant yet!'

She stood up, her legs still feeling shaky. 'I'm going——'

His hand was painful on her wrist, deliberately so, she felt. 'You aren't going anywhere, not until this thing is settled.'

'It is settled as far as I'm concerned——'

'Until you want to claim paternity,' he said bitterly.

Rachel felt as if someone had knocked the breath from her body. 'I—You—We have no reason to suppose——'

'We have no reason *not* to suppose either,' he snarled. 'Do we?'

'I don't—I—You . . .?'

'*I* didn't do anything to prevent it. And by the very fact that you were a virgin neither did you. Unless of course you planned ahead,' his mouth twisted. 'Did you? Did you plan to lose your virginity to a famous tennis star?'

'No!'

'Then you'll marry me! No child of mine is going to grow up thinking I don't want it—I had enough of that in my own childhood. But I'll make you pay for your damned stupidity. I made enough comments about spending the night with you!' he added disgustedly.

She had paled at the vehemence in his voice, the glitter of anger in his eyes, swallowing hard. 'You won't see me again to make me *pay* for anything——'

'I hope you don't think I intend dealing with this through a lawyer as my father did——'

'Dealing with *what*?' she said angrily, not concerned with his own family. 'There's nothing *to* deal with. We made a mistake, let that be the end of it.'

'But it isn't, is it?' he muttered, his mouth a thin angry line. 'There could be a baby, you know that— *my* baby.'

A baby, a child made between herself and Nick. Strangely the thought didn't frighten her as it would a lot of girls in the same predicament. Her parents loved her, and although they might be shocked in the beginning, she had no doubt they would stand by her. But what of the baby's father? Nick didn't act the sort of man who would simply ignore the existence of his own child, hadn't he assured her that he wouldn't?

But the possibility of there being a child was extremely remote! Nick was jumping to conclusions.

'We've only done it once——'

His hard laugh interrupted her. 'I wonder how many times a doctor has heard that after confirming a girl's pregnancy,' he scorned. 'Don't be naïve, Rachel. It only takes the once.'

She blushed in spite of herself. 'I wouldn't make any claims on you——'

'I'm sure my mother told my father the same thing— before slapping him with a lawsuit,' he scorned once again.

'I wouldn't do that!' she gasped, wondering just what sort of parents he had.

'You won't get the chance,' he snapped. 'Once we're married——'

'Married?' she echoed sharply. 'I'm not marrying you!'

Nick came to stand in front of her, looking down at

her pityingly. 'Any child of mine that you bring into this world will have me as its legal father.'

'No!' Rachel cried her agitation, pushing past Nick as he would have stopped her. 'I'm not marrying you for any reason!'

'You'll marry me,' he told her grimly. 'I'll see to it.'

'Never!' she turned on him vehemently. 'You can't make me marry you, and I would never do it voluntarily.'

'I've said you'll marry me, Rachel, and you will.'

'Why can't you wait?' two bright spots of colour heightened her cheeks. 'We would know in a few weeks.'

'And so would everyone else, including the child when it was old enough to realise we were married only six or seven months before it was born. Being illegitimate myself I know exactly how it feels to have that stigma attached to you. And no child of mine is going to go through what I did.'

'Always supposing there was a child.'

'I'm not prepared to take the risk that there isn't,' he snapped.

'Well, I am!' Rachel marched through to the lounge to pick up her handbag. 'I don't even want to see you again, let alone marry you. Goodbye!' She slammed out of the apartment, all the time she was running down the stairs expecting to hear Nick's pounding footsteps behind her. As she stepped out on to the pavement she knew he had not followed her, and breathed a sigh of relief as she hailed a taxi, giving her address as she climbed inside.

She leant her head back against the seat, staring sightlessly up at the roof. Minutes ago Nick St Clare had made love to her! He had offered to make her his wife, had insisted on it because of some hurt in his own childhood, but what sort of marriage would that have been?

She daren't even begin to probe the way she had offered no resistance to his lovemaking, daren't begin to guess her feelings towards him. She only knew that tonight had been a mistake, a mistake Nick seemed intent on making her pay for the rest of her life.

Could one really get pregnant as easily as that? A few brief minutes of forgetfulness, of years of inborn restraint ignored for a short time, and she could suffer the consequences for a lifetime. Nick was right, she was being naïve thinking she couldn't become pregnant from tonight. Once was all it took, just once . . .

Her parents were still up when she got in, and somehow she managed to act normally enough with them to escape to her bedroom without alerting their suspicions as to how upset she was. Her explanation that she had met Nick and spent the evening with him was readily accepted, and she left to go to bed on the excuse that she was tired.

Once in her room she lay in the darkness, fully clothed, starring into space. She could be carrying Nick's child, a child he wanted, could even now be forging a new life inside her, a life from her and Nick's brief lovemaking. No child should be made from such a union, any baby deserved better than that, and Nick obviously thought so too; the bitterness connected with his own childhood was obvious. If it were true that he was illegitimate himself then his determination was easily understood.

Rachel turned her face into the pillow, sobs finally racking her body. What had she done—what had she done!

He had assumed she knew what she was doing, had thought she realised he wanted to sleep with her. As he said, he had made enough remarks about her spending the night with him!

She was deathly white as she went to college the next morning, knowing she had to go or arouse her mother's concern.

She hadn't slept at all, the threat of Nick St Clare hovering on the borders of her mind even when she wasn't consciously thinking about him, his presence looming like a black shadow in her life, and there was another even more worrying shadow that she wouldn't even let begin take shape in her mind.

'You look awful,' came Hilary's cheerful greeting as they met in the corridor on their way to their first class.

'Thanks!' Rachel accepted dully.

'You look as if you spent a night on the tiles.'

She ignored her friend's questioning tone, continuing on their way to the classroom.

'Rachel?'

'Yes?' Her voice was lifeless.

'Is there anything wrong?' Hilary's teasing had gone now.

'No, nothing,' she answered stiltedly.

Her friend frowned. 'You don't look well.'

'I don't feel well.'

'Headache?'

'I—Yes.' After all, she did have a throb at her temples, mainly through lack of sleep, but it was still a headache.

Hilary began searching through her handbag. 'I think I have some aspirin——'

'I've already taken some,' Rachel refused the medication, knowing that she daren't risk taking anything like that until she was sure she wasn't pregnant.

Hilary sat down at the desk next to her. 'Are you upset because Nick St Clare lost yesterday?' She seemed puzzled and disturbed by Rachel's distant manner.

The tennis match, the playing of it, Nick's losing, his disappointment, seemed to have happened years ago. She certainly hadn't given it a thought after what had happened later. 'Someone has to lose,' she said woodenly.

'Yes, but——'

'Mr Adams wants to start the class,' she warned as the tutor looked at them both pointedly.

As far as she was concerned Mr Adams might have been talking in Russian for all that she understood or took in any of what he said. She couldn't concentrate on anything; she was starting to feel numb, both her mind and her emotions. Admittedly the world didn't look quite so black this morning. After all, there might not be a baby, and Nick certainly couldn't force her to do anything she didn't want to do. And she didn't want to be his wife! She felt sure that once he had calmed down, thought about this rationally, he wouldn't want that either.

'Where's your big-shot tennis player now?' taunted a familiar voice as she stared down into her cooling coffee.

Rachel looked up at Danny with dull eyes. She and Hilary had been seated in the canteen for the last ten minutes, and so far she hadn't spoken a word, and to Hilary's credit she hadn't spoken either, respecting her wish for silence.

Danny pulled a chair over from another table, turning it towards him, resting his arms along the back as he straddled it. 'Lost, didn't he?' he mocked, a smile of satisfaction to his lips.

Rachel looked at him coldly, wondering, and far from the first time, what she had ever seen in him. Maybe she had felt flattered that such a popular boy should be interested in her; it certainly hadn't been his pleasant nature that had attracted her.

'I suppose that was his girl-friend sitting next to you,' he taunted.

Rachel's eyes chilled even more. Danny really was a bad loser, vindictively so.

'She was really beautiful,' he added with relish. 'Sophisticated too.'

She was aware of that. Probably Suzy Freeman had enough sense not to make the mistake she had last night too. Just to think of it made her pale.

'Put you in the shade, didn't she?' Danny continued nastily.

Hilary took one look at Rachel's pale face and turned on Danny. 'Why don't you go away?' she snapped. 'Go and amuse your little friends,' she looked over at the waiting Billy and Malcolm. 'Because we certainly aren't amused!'

His face darkened with anger. 'Who rang your bell?' he snarled.

'And who opened your cage?' she returned sweetly.

'Why, you little——'

'Please stop,' Rachel sighed wearily, 'both of you. Let's go, Hilary,' and she stood up.

Danny looked up with a sneer. 'Didn't last very long, did you?' he mocked.

'Drop dead!' Hilary snapped.

His mocking laughter followed them from the room. Rachel had no idea how she was going to get through the rest of the day, wishing she could just crawl into bed and sleep until this mess was over, one way or the other. The next couple of months were really going to drag.

'Cheer up,' Hilary encouraged gently. 'I'm sure it can't be that bad.'

'It's worse!' Rachel's shoulders drooped dejectedly.

'Want to tell me?'

'Not really,' she shook her head regretfully. 'But thanks, anyway, Hilary.'

Her friend shrugged. 'Any time you need a shoulder to cry on . . .'

'I'll come to you.' She gave a wan smile.

That time could come all too soon! She had been so naïve, so trusting, that it hadn't occurred to her that when Nick said he needed her, that he wanted to be with her last night, that he had meant *all* night.

And if her worst fears should be realised, if there should be a baby, she would have the terrible job of telling her parents. Not that she had any doubts about their support, but she would still have to tell them.

Somehow she got through the day, although if the next few weeks continued as badly as today she was going to fail her end-of-year exams in a couple of weeks.

'This ought to cheer you up,' Hilary whispered as they left the college that evening.

'Mm?' Rachel answered her friend vaguely.

'Look over there!' Hilary said excitedly.

She followed her friend's line of vision, stiffening as she recognised Nick leaning against the red Jaguar. He seemed to see her at about the same time, and straightened away from the car to come towards her, his expression grim.

Her first instinct was to turn and run, but pride took over and she stood her ground, eyeing him defiantly. If he was here for a fight then she was ready for him!

'Hilary,' he spoke to her friend first.

'Mr St Clare,' she answered excitedly.

Now he turned to Rachel, his eyes narrowed to blue slits. 'Are you ready to leave?' he asked her coldly.

'I——'

'Perhaps we can give you a lift today, Hilary?' Once again he ignored Rachel.

'Yes, please,' she accepted eagerly.

'Rachel?' His voice cooled.

He had put her in a position where she couldn't refuse—and he knew it! 'Ready,' she accepted distantly. 'Hilary and I have some work to go through together, so if you could just drop us both off at her house?' She ignored her friend's gaping look, meeting Nick's gaze unflinchingly.

He opened the car door for her and Hilary to get in. 'Your parents are expecting us,' he returned smoothly, slamming the door after her before going round to get in behind the wheel.

Rachel suddenly felt breathless, turning to him anxiously as he started the engine with a roar. 'My parents?' she demanded worriedly.

'Yes,' he answered abruptly, shooting a warning look in Hilary's direction.

She bit her lip, realising the need for caution. 'You've seen my parents?'

He nodded. 'I've just left them.'

Heavens, if he had said anything to them . . .! But he wouldn't have done. He must have just gone to see her and as before they had told him she was at college.

Nevertheless, she waited impatiently for the time when they were alone, wanting to know exactly what had been said when he met her parents earlier.

'See you on Monday,' she told Hilary absently as her friend got out out of the car.

Nick's expression was forbidding as they drove on

to her home, the easy charm with which he had spoken
to Hilary a few minutes earlier completely disappearing.

'Mr St Clare——' Rachel began.

'Your formality is going to sound rather stupid when
we get to your home,' he mocked harshly.

'I—Why?' she asked warily.

He shot her a look of indifference. 'Because your
parents are eagerly awaiting our return so that they
can begin organising the wedding.'

CHAPTER FIVE

'WHAT do you mean?' she gasped, her hands beginning to shake, her face taking on a sickly pallor.

Nick shrugged. 'You didn't seem to have told your parents we were getting married, so I took it upon myself to inform them.'

'No . . .' she gave a weak cry of protest, the nightmare of yesterday now taking on terrifying proportions. 'You had no right! I told you I wouldn't marry you——'

'And I told you that you would,' he said grimly.

She swallowed hard. 'My parents—what did they say?' Her eyes were huge in her pale face.

'They were surprised——'

'Surprised!' she choked. 'I'm sure they were more than that.'

'A little disappointed too,' Nick nodded. 'That you hadn't told them yourself.'

'It isn't the sort of thing one discusses over a cup of coffee,' she said bitterly, looking down at her hands, tears in her eyes.

His mouth tightened. 'Just what do you think I've told your parents?' he snapped.

Two bright spots of colour appeared in her cheeks. 'I—You——'

'I haven't told them I made love to you, if that's what you think,' he rasped.

Hope shone in her smoky-grey eyes. 'You haven't?'

'Of course I damn well haven't,' he said angrily, his jaw rigid. 'The fewer people who know about that the better.'

Rachel licked her lips, becoming more and more confused by the minute. 'Then what did you tell them?' she frowned.

His mouth twisted. 'That you and I are in love, that we want to be married before my tournament in Boston.'

'But that isn't true!'

He shot her a contemptuous glance. 'Your parents are very nice people, I think they would be a little shocked by the truth.'

'No more shocked than they would be by that lie!' Rachel's eyes flashed.

'No?' he quirked one dark blond eyebrow. 'Your parents think of you as their sweet innocent little girl,' he taunted. 'It wouldn't even occur to them that you could have slept with a complete stranger.'

'I—It just happened.' She shook her head. 'I don't want to marry you.'

'Oh, I know that,' he laughed without humour. 'But as I told you last night, you have no choice. A lot of men in my position might be prepared to take the risk, to pay up if necessary, but not me. I won't have that for my child! I *want* this baby. You would have known my reaction if you'd known me better.'

'I think you're mad,' she told him angrily. 'What happened last night—happened. We don't have to get married because of it.'

'Don't think I *want* you for my wife——'

'Thank you!' she snapped.

'Because I don't,' he continued harshly.

'And I don't want you!'

'No,' he acknowledged hardly. 'But it's too late now. Much too late,' he added softly.

Rachel could see there was no arguing with him.

Nothing she said would convince him not to marry her. He was a determined man, and that determination had something to do with the parents he kept referring to so bitterly.

'My parents won't believe we've fallen in love with each other,' she mumbled.

'They'd better,' Nick said grimly.

'But they won't,' she sighed. 'Love doesn't happen this way. We met four days ago——'

'And your parents were married a week after their first meeting,' he told her calmly.

'They weren't!' she gasped.

Nick eyed her frowningly, a glint of humour in his deep blue eyes. 'Didn't you know that?'

'No . . .'

'Well, they were. Of course they were a little concerned about the fact that you're only eighteen—your mother was in her twenties when they fell in love so suddenly—but I soon convinced them that we're so deeply in love that we just can't wait to get married, that I want to marry you before I leave for Boston next week.'

'Next week?' she squeaked.

'Yes,' he confirmed tersely.

'But I can't marry you next week!'

'You *will* marry me next week,' Nick said arrogantly, stopping the car outside her home before turning in his seat to look at her. 'I'm not going to argue with you about this, Rachel, especially not in front of your parents. It would only upset them to know the truth, I'm sure you realise that?'

She was trapped, Nick knew it, and so did she. But *next week*! She couldn't become this man's wife next week or any other time.

'They would understand——'

'No!' Nick's voice was harsh. 'Not when I tell them I love you and *want* to marry you. This is the way it has to be, Rachel. And maybe you won't find it so bad.' He was suddenly dangerously, seductively close.

Rachel fought the magnetism of that seduction. She had fallen for it once, but not again.

Nick's hand gently touched her parted lips, his thumb-tip moving erotically against their softness. 'After all,' he murmured throatily, 'marriage does have its compensations.'

Her breathing was suddenly ragged. 'It does?' Her voice was husky.

'Oh yes,' he nodded, his head lowering as his mouth took possession of hers.

For all her resolve not to respond to him, for all her certainty that she hated him, she melted against him at the first touch of his lips, and heard a faint groan in his throat before he pulled her fiercely against him, devouring her mouth with a savagery that took both their breaths away.

They were both breathing deeply by the time they broke apart. 'Yes,' Nick murmured, 'it has its compensations.'

Rachel was fast trying to gather her scattered wits. 'And if I'm not pregnant?'

His face became a harsh mask, deep lines etched beside his nose and mouth, as he thrust her away from him. 'Then you get right back out of my life!' he rasped.

She flinched as if he had hit her, feeling sick at the vehemence in his face. Nick hated her, really hated her.

'You look surprised,' he scorned. 'What did you expect, a declaration to love you no matter what?'

'No——'

'Maybe that's as well,' he swung out of the car, coming round to open her door for her, 'because you'll never get one from me.' He kept a tight grip on her elbow as they went down the pathway to the house. 'Your parents believe us to be in love, I hope you don't do anything to make them doubt that.'

The words were a warning, not that she needed them; she was too numb to do anything but accept her mother and father's warm hugs of congratulations.

'Although we tried to persuade Mr St Clare—Nick,' her father amended at the other man's look of displeasure, 'we tried to persuade him to wait a while, give you both time to see if this is really what you want.'

'I——'

Nick's arm came possessively about her shoulders. 'We already know what we want. We want to belong to each other, don't we, sweetheart?' he looked down at Rachel.

'Er—yes,' she agreed huskily.

'But it's such short notice, dear,' her mother fussed. 'And you have your exams in two weeks' time.'

Rachel had forgotten all about the end-of-the-year exams!

'I trust you aren't one of these young men who disapprove of women having a career?' Her father looked sternly at Nick.

'Rachel must do whatever she thinks best,' he answered stiffly.

She knew what answer she was supposed to make, knew what Nick was silently willing her to say, and yet she couldn't say it. Here was a way for her to get out of being with Nick, and she intended taking it.

'I think I'd like to do the exams,' she said clearly.

'Of course it means we'll have to delay the wedding——'

'No!' Nick cut in firmly.

'No?' She looked at him uncertainly.

He shook his head, a warning glitter to his eyes. 'Stay here and take your exams by all means, I'll be pretty busy in Boston anyway. But the wedding will take place before I leave.'

'Oh, but——'

'Surely——'

'It's what we both want, isn't it, honey?' he prompted hardly, his fingers biting into her flesh.

'I—Yes.' The pressure eased on her shoulder.

Her father frowned at her hesitation. 'If you aren't sure, Rachel, now is the time to say so—not after the wedding,' he added lightly at Nick's dark scowl. 'You haven't known each other long——'

'Nick says you and Mummy only knew each other a week before you were married.' Rachel still found this hard to believe. Her parents had always seemed so staid to her, every move, every decision, methodically thought out, that it seemed totally out of character to her that they should have acted so impetuously.

Her father looked abashed. 'We had no doubts, and your grandparents were emigrating to Australia. We didn't have a lot of time to think about it.'

'We feel the same way,' Nick told him.

'Ah, but you're coming back——'

'We want to be together now,' Nick said firmly. 'I hope you understand, Mr James,' his voice softened, became persuasive rather than demanding. 'We want to do what's right, don't want to act impetuously, that's why the wedding has to be straight away.'

Her father flushed at the clear meaning behind Nick's words. 'Rachel is very young,' he said sternly.

'But you're a man of the world, surely able to control the situation.'

Rachel was feeling very uncomfortable by this time, very embarrassed by the intimate turn of the conversation in front of her parents. How much more embarrassed she would have been if they had to be told she and Nick had already made love!

The look Nick shot down at her was openly mocking, the expression quickly masked as once again he spoke to her father. 'It's purely because I am a man of the world that I know how dangerous this situation could be.'

'I see,' her father pursed his lips. 'Rachel?'

'I——' Once again Nick's fingers dug warningly into her flesh. 'Nick and I want to get married,' she said softly, looking down at her hands.

'If you're sure . . .?'

She met her father's gaze steadily. 'I am.'

He visibly relaxed. 'Then we'd better start arranging the wedding,' he smiled.

Nick was triumphant as he looked down at her, and as the arrangements began to be discussed it became obvious that he already had most of it organised.

'I never had a choice, did I?' Rachel said bitterly as she walked him to his car a short time later, Nick having refused to stay to dinner, claiming a previous appointment with his coach.

'No,' he acknowledged grimly. 'I'll pick you up at seven o'clock and we'll go and see Kay, tell her the happy news.'

She flinched at his contemptuous tone. 'All right.'

Nick's eyes narrowed on her pale face. 'You don't look well.'

'I don't feel well.'

His mouth twisted derisively. 'It's too early for morning sickness!'

'I doubt I'll have it,' she flashed. 'I doubt I'm pregnant.'

'Then you'll be able to divorce me, won't you?'

'I'll get an annulment.'

'No way, Rachel,' he scorned. 'I may have to marry you, but I'm certainly not forgoing all the—pleasures of married life.'

She swallowed hard. 'You would expect a normal marriage?'

'Of course. And you're a fool if you expected anything else.'

She hadn't even thought about it, that side of the marriage had not even occurred to her. 'I don't think——'

'You won't have to,' Nick taunted.

Rachel flushed. 'I hope I'm not pregnant!' she told him vehemently.

'So do I,' he said bitterly. 'Believe me, so do I. Now maybe you'd better kiss me goodbye. And before you refuse I think you should know that your parents are standing at the window watching us. No, don't look,' he commanded at her involuntary movement. 'The kiss, Rachel,' he reminded her. 'For your brand-new fiancé.'

She had no choice, but she hated Nick's manipulation of her as she stood on tiptoe to kiss him briefly on the lips.

'Not very convincing,' he taunted as she moved away.

'It will have to do,' she snapped moodily. 'I would hardly go into a passionate clinch in the middle of the street!'

'No, you save your passion for the bedroom, don't you?' He gave a humourless smile as she paled. 'I'll see you at seven o'clock.'

Rachel walked slowly back into the house, dreading the next few minutes with her parents. But she needn't have worried, they seemed convinced of the fact that she and Nick were deeply in love.

His sister seemed convinced of it too when they visited her later that evening, she was very excited at the thought of her brother getting married.

'I didn't think he would ever take the plunge,' she confided teasingly.

'I doubt I would have done if I hadn't met Rachel,' Nick drawled.

'I never thought my big brother would admit to love at first sight!'

Rachel knew he was far from admitting that. Nick despised her for this enforced marriage, and he lost no opportunity to let her know that, taking digs at her whenever he got the chance.

'Rachel is an original,' he told his sister. 'I've never met anyone quite like her before.'

'And to think Eve and I brought you together!' Kay smiled.

'Oh, I think Rachel and I would have met anyway,' he said dryly.

'Fate, you mean?'

'Something like that,' he mocked.

Rachel flushed uncomfortably. Nick might be bitter, but if he thought she wanted this marriage any more than he did then he was mistaken!

'I never knew you were a romantic, Nick,' his sister said delightedly, obviously enjoying seeing her brother apparently bowed by love.

'Neither did I,' his voice was harsh now. 'Where's Richard?' He changed the subject, seemingly tired of this veiled baiting of Rachel.

How Rachel got through the next few days she never

knew, although a lot of her time was spent looking for her wedding dress and making reception arrangements. She went to college as normal, while Nick took care of the actual ceremony, his manner coolly polite now, a little warmer in front of her parents, but not much more. Her parents seemed to put his behaviour down to restraint, even seemed to admire him for it.

The only argument they had in the days preceding the wedding came when Rachel told him she had definitely decided to stay in England while he went to Boston.

'You know damn well I only agreed to that in front of your parents,' Nick scowled. 'I have no intention of going to Boston and leaving my wife in England.'

The two of them were spending the evening before the wedding at Nick's flat, the first time they had really spent alone since they had made love.

'I want to take my exams,' Rachel said stubbornly.

'But they aren't important. As my wife——'

'I may not be your wife for longer than the summer,' she reminded him.

His mouth twisted. 'And if you aren't you intend going on with your career?'

'Of course.'

'Life has to go on, and all that.'

'Yes,' she flushed.

'And in the meantime I have to be without my wife!'

'You said yourself that you wouldn't have time for me in Boston——'

'I'd make time—for this.' He pulled her roughly into his arms, his eyes glittering down at her in challenge before his mouth moved possessively over hers. He didn't ask for a response, didn't even seem to want one as his lips plundered hers, his hands moving knowledgeably over her body, searching out her heaving

Yours FREE with a home subscription to
SUPERROMANCES™

Now you never have to
miss reading the newest
SUPERROMANCES...
because they'll be delivered
right to your door.
   Start with your free
Love beyond Desire. You'll
be enthralled by this
powerful love story...from
the moment Robin meets
the dark, handsome Carlos and
finds herself involved in the jealousies, bitterness
and secret passions of the Lopez family. Where her
own forbidden love threatens to shatter her life.

   Your free *Love beyond Desire* is only the
beginning. A subscription to **SUPERROMANCE** lets
you look forward to a long love affair. Month after
month, you'll receive four love stories of heroic
dimension. Novels that will involve you in spellbinding
intrigue, forbidden love and fiery passions.
   You'll begin this series of sensuous, exciting
contemporary novels...written by some of the top
romance novelists of the day...with four every month.
   And this big value...each novel, almost 400
pages of compelling reading...is yours for only $2.50
a book. Hours of entertainment every month for so
little. Far less than a first-run movie or pay-TV. Newly
published novels, with beautifully illustrated covers,
filled with page after page of delicious escape into a
world of romantic love...delivered right to your home.

A compelling love story of mystery and intrigue... conflicts and jealousies... and a forbidden love that threatens to shatter the lives of all involved with the aristocratic Lopez family.

⌐ Mail this card today for your FREE gifts.

TAKE THIS BOOK
AND TOTE BAG **FREE!**

Mail to: **SUPERROMANCE**
649 Ontario Street, Stratford Ontario N5A 6W2

YES, please send me FREE and without any obligation, my SUPERROMANCE novel, *Love Beyond Desire*. If you do not hear from me after I have examined my FREE book, please send me the 4 new SUPERROMANCE books every month as soon as they come off the press. I understand that I will be billed only $2.50 per book (total $10.00). There are no shipping and handling or any other hidden charges. There is no minimum number of books that I have to purchase. In fact, I may cancel this arrangement at any time. *Love Beyond Desire* and the tote bag are mine to keep as FREE gifts even if I do not buy any additional books.

334-CIS-YKB4

Name	(Please Print)
Address	Apt. No.
City	
Province	Postal Code
Signature	(If under 18, parent or guardian must sign.)

This offer is limited to one order per household and not valid to present subscribers.
We reserve the right to exercise discretion in granting membership. If price changes are necessary you will be notified. Offer expires September 30, 1983.

PRINTED IN U.S.A.   **SUPERROMANCE**

breasts, probing the neckline of her blouse to capture one of them in his hands.

His other hand moved up to unbutton the blouse, pushing it aside to reveal the lacy half-cups of her flesh-coloured bra, her breasts swelling temptingly as Nick's head lowered, his lips heated against her skin.

She didn't want this, couldn't let it happen. And yet she couldn't stop it either; her hands were in the golden thickness of his hair as she held him to her, she gasped her pleasure as he possessed one taut nipple with the moist warmth of his mouth and tongue.

It was all happening as it had last time—Nick was bending to pick her up. 'No!' she cried, pulling away from him.

For a moment he looked dazed, then he straightened. 'No,' he agreed derisively, pushing her shaking hands away to finish the task of buttoning her blouse. 'But I'd make time for that in Boston, Rachel,' he drawled mockingly.

She turned away, her movements jerky. 'I'm not going.'

He spun her round, his expression vicious. 'I want you there!'

'And I don't want to go,' she said dully.

'Why?' he demanded harshly. 'I can assure you that our—marriage would not be impaired by my playing.'

Delicate colour flooded her cheeks. But she knew she deserved his derision. She had responded to him, encouraged him, and he had been the one who regained control first after she had pulled away from him, her senses were still reeling, if she dared to admit it.

'Those exams are important to me——'

'More important than me?'

As quickly as the colour had entered her cheeks it now left them, leaving her white with tension, her eyes deeply grey. Had Nick guessed her secret? Could he possibly know the terrible secret she was frightened to admit even to herself? The anger in his face seemed to say no and she breathed easily again, knowing that once again the nameless fear didn't have to be faced.

'Do I need to answer that?' she scorned.

Rage blazed in the dark blue eyes. 'I swear, if you stay my wife I'll make you sorry for this!'

'So you've already said,' she answered calmly.

'All right,' he snapped. 'Stay here! Two nights with you should be enough anyway.'

Rachel gave him a startled look. 'You leave Saturday?'

'First thing,' he nodded.

'I—And will you be in Boston long?'

'About a week. Then I go to Washington.'

'And then?' She held her breath as she waited for his answer.

His mouth twisted. 'Then I come home to you, sweet wife.'

'When?' she asked woodenly.

Nick shrugged. 'About the twenty-sixth of July. Helpful?' he quirked a mocking eyebrow.

'No,' she flushed.

'Well, I leave again at the beginning of August, so we should know something by then.'

'Not necessarily,' Rachel said stiffly. 'It usually takes eight to ten weeks to confirm it.'

He nodded. 'Maybe when I'm through the U.S. Open.'

'Do you play tennis all year long?' she snapped irritably.

'If I want to. I take the odd week off here and there, but otherwise it's a full calendar.'

'And you enjoy it.'

'Yes.'

'No more thoughts of retiring?' She was amazed that they actually seemed to be having a normal conversation!

Nick grimaced. 'I was on a downer, as Kay pointed out. Most people are when they've just lost an important match like that one. Wimbledon is the big one, and I wanted to win it once before I retired.'

'You have time——'

'Not much more. How will you like being married to a has been?' he taunted, effectively ending any politeness between them.

'I hope I'm not going to be married to anyone!' Rachel snapped.

Nick pulled on his jacket with savage movements. 'I'd better get you home, we have a busy day tomorrow.'

She pulled on her own coat. 'Trying to impress my parents again, Nick?' she mocked.

He gave an unwilling smile. 'They do rather like me, don't they?'

She quirked a mocking eyebrow. 'Weren't they supposed to?'

He was grinning openly now, picking up his car keys. 'That was the general idea.'

'Why?' She followed him outside, going down to the car.

'It's usual to get on with one's in-laws—or, at least, try to.'

Nick had gone out of his way to be pleasant and charming to her parents, so much so that they had nothing but praise for him. In the end she just shut herself off during their praising of him, knowing that beneath the charm was a cruel streak, a harshness that he felt no compunction about showing her.

But his charm was the only thing in evidence the next day as they were quietly married. It was a lunch-time wedding, with only about thirty people present at the reception held at Rachel's parents' home afterwards. Only a few of the guests were actually Nick's, just his sister, her husband and baby, and Suzy and Sam Freeman; the other people were all friends or relatives of Rachel's.

'You can't get married without the close family present,' her mother had protested when Rachel said she would rather there were no guests. 'Otherwise they'll think we have something to hide.'

Rachel blushed. 'That's ridiculous! I've only known Nick a week!'

Her mother had wiped a tear from her eyes. 'My little girl getting married!'

Rachel's expression softened. 'I'm not exactly going away, Nick's apartment isn't far from here.'

'No doubt you'll start travelling with him later on.'

'No doubt.' She had changed the subject after that, accepting that her immediate family at least had to witness the marriage. If only there weren't so many of them!

A dazed Hilary had been invited too, in fact she came along on Thursday morning to help Rachel dress.

'It's a beautiful dress,' she said wistfully as she helped Rachel into it.

Rachel looked at her reflection in the mirror. 'Even though it's only a register office wedding my parents insisted I had to wear white,' she explained ruefully. The white chiffon gown was not a traditional wedding dress, but more like a cocktail dress, high-necked, and fitted over her bust and waist, falling in soft folds to just below her knee. A white pillbox hat on her dark gleaming hair, and a small posy of yellow carnations, would complete the outfit.

'And Nick?' Hilary began to secure long dark hair on top of Rachel's head.

She grimaced. 'He agreed with them.' Much to her surprise he had insisted she wear white too.

'You're so lucky, Rachel,' her friend gave an envious sigh. 'Nick St Clare as your husband!'

A shutter came down over her emotions. 'Yes.'

'I don't know how you can bear to let him go away without you.'

'I have to take my exams,' Rachel explained.

'But you won't need them!' Hilary shook her head. 'I think you're mad!'

'Wouldn't you say getting married this quickly is madder?' Rachel gave a wan smile.

'Not if you're in love.'

'You're an incurable romantic,' she teased. And she had been cured for life!

Hilary halted her task, frowning down at her. 'You are in love, aren't you?'

Rachel licked her suddenly dry lips. 'I——'

'Of course you are,' luckily Hilary answered her own question. 'I wish someone handsome and exciting would come along and sweep *me* off my feet!'

Rachel had to laugh at her friend's woebegone expression, and the tension she had been under all morning lessened slightly.

But it came back with a vengeance the moment she set eyes on Nick at the register office. He looked so distinguished in the dark pin-striped suit, his hair golden against its dark colour, but his eyes were cold as he looked back at her.

'You look beautiful,' Kay told her, the sleeping Eve in her arms. 'Doesn't she, Nick?'

'Very,' he agreed tersely. 'Shall we go in?'

As Rachel moved to stand beside him her attention was caught and held be vehement blue eyes. Suzy Freeman was looking at her with open dislike, a sneer to her lips as she continued to stare.

Rachel turned away, more unnerved than she cared to admit, hardly aware of the ceremony taking place as she felt blue eyes boring into her back. Suzy Freeman hated her, and there could be no doubting the reason why she did.

'Rachel!' Nick prompted harshly.

She looked up to find the registrar watching her expectantly. She looked frantically to Nick for help.

'I do,' he prompted in a fierce whisper.

Heavens, had the ceremony got that far already! She swallowed hard. 'I do,' she said in a strained voice.

Within minutes, it seemed, the kindly man standing in front of her pronounced them man and wife.

'You may kiss the bride,' he beamed down at them.

'With pleasure,' Nick growled, his head swooping as his mouth took possession of hers.

It was as if he were punishing her for her attention wandering; the kiss went on and on, not at all like the small kiss of celebration they had been invited to take. Finally Rachel struggled to be released.

Nick's eyes glittered down at her. 'Mrs St Clare,' he said in a sneer.

Her mouth felt numb from the fierce pressure of his, although she managed a shaky smile as family and friends came forward to congratulate them.

The small reception was being held at her parents' home. The furniture had been moved back in the large lounge to accommodate the thirty or so guests, and a buffet lunch was laid out on a table set against one wall.

Rachel and Nick stood just inside the room welcoming the guests as they came in, neither of them having spoken a word to each other since Nick had so cruelly taunted her about being Mrs St Clare.

She felt herself tense as Suzy Freeman and her father came towards them, and Nick looked at them too as her tension was relayed to him by his impersonal hold on her elbow.

Sam Freeman's congratulations were warm and sincerely meant, then he was taken by her mother to be introduced to some of the other guests.

Suzy Freeman looked at Rachel with open contempt, her gaze warming as she turned to Nick. 'Do I congratulate or commiserate with you?' she drawled.

Rachel gasped at this open attack, although Nick seemed unperturbed; he grinned widely, accepting the other woman's lingering kiss on the lips with an equal response.

'Only time will tell,' he taunted.

Icy blue eyes were once again levelled on Rachel. 'You're certainly to be congratulated.' Suzy's mouth twisted. 'And I do congratulate you, Miss James.'

'Mrs St Clare,' she corrected stiffly.

'Not for long, I trust,' Suzy Freeman scorned before once more kissing Nick on the mouth. 'I'll see you soon, darling.'

Nick was smiling openly by this time, obviously having enjoyed the other woman's attention.

'What did she mean by that?' Rachel asked through stiff lips.

He shrugged, sipping the champagne they had all been given as they came into the room. 'Suzy will naturally be coming to Boston with Sam and me.'

It was the first Rachel had heard of it, but that wasn't what was troubling her. 'What did she mean about my not being Mrs St Clare for long?' she asked.

'Nick,' her father joined them, 'come and say hello to Rachel's grandparents. And there's a dozen or so aunts and uncles who would like to meet you too,' he teased.

'Of course, Jim,' Nick agreed instantly. 'You'll be all right, Rachel?'

'Yes,' she answered distantly.

Her father mistook her reserve for disappointment. 'Don't worry, love,' he squeezed her hand, 'I'll bring him back as soon as I can!'

Nick's eyes mocked her as he kissed her lightly on the lips. 'I won't be long, honey,' he taunted.

Rachel watched him as he moved around the room charming and flattering members of her family, knowing that he had captivated them all within a few minutes of being introduced. Everyone appeared to be having a good time, her mother was in her element as hostess, Kay and Richard were talking to Hilary, Sam Freeman was now in conversation with her father as Nick took one of her little cousins on to his knee, and the five-year-old giggled as he whispered something in her ear.

'He's wonderful with children, isn't he?' a female voice taunted at her side.

She turned wavy grey eyes on Suzy Freeman. 'Yes,' she replied stiltedly.

The other woman's mouth twisted. 'But then he could need to be, couldn't he?' she scorned.

Rachel paled. 'What do you mean?'

Suzy gave her a contemptuous look. 'You think Nick didn't tell us about your scheming?'

She swallowed hard. 'I don't know, did he?'

'Of course,' the other woman nodded. 'Nick doesn't keep much from me, especially as we had plans to marry ourselves.'

Rachel felt as if the ground were fast disappearing from beneath her feet. 'I—If you'll excuse me, I think I'll go out into the garden. I need some air.'

'What a good idea,' Suzy said smoothly. 'It is a little warm in here.'

The last thing Rachel wanted was for Suzy Freeman to come with her. She needed time to collect her thoughts together, to accept that part of Nick's anger was due to the fact that he believed her to have prevented him marrying the woman he really wanted.

Suzy walked at her side as they moved around the large garden. 'Nick's always been such a flirt,' she mused. 'But I accepted that. And he knew that when he was ready to settle down I would be waiting. He always felt I was too young for marriage yet,' she added ruefully. 'So what he's going to do with a child bride I have no idea.'

Rachel looked at her with dull eyes. 'Don't you?'

Once again the hatred came back into Suzy's face. 'Oh, no doubt you'll prove amusing for a while. Until you became big with his child,' she added with vehemence. 'Have no doubt who he'll turn to then. And I'll be waiting, Rachel, as I always have.'

She had sensed this woman was an enemy the last time they had met, and now she knew it. Suzy would feel no compunction about sleeping with Nick, even if he did have a wife and child.

'Maybe you won't have to wait long,' she said tautly. 'If there isn't a child he could be yours' again in two months.'

They walked on in silence for several minutes, the light breeze exactly what Rachel needed to revive her. This conversation would have been unpleasant at any time, but at least out here there could be no witnesses to her humiliation. Nick must have known his mistress would talk to her like this, and he had done nothing to prevent it.

'You were very clever, of course,' Suzy stopped to admire the roses, 'although perhaps a little silly too.'

'Oh yes?'

'Nick hates deception of any sort, he always has.'

'Might I remind you that he was there too, the night we—we—Well, he was there too,' Rachel finished angrily.

'Of course,' Suzy drawled. 'Otherwise he wouldn't need to be *here* now. I've waited a long time for Nick to get married, and now it's to someone else. But considering the reason he's marrying you I'm glad it isn't me. God, I could have pulled the same trick on him hundreds of times if I'd been that desperate for marriage. But I know how he must hate you for tricking him into this marriage.'

She couldn't have told Rachel any more clearly how close she and Nick were, and for some time, by the sound of it.

'Why would he hate me?' Rachel asked softly, realising that Nick's background might now be explained to her, his claim to being illegitimate.

Suzy looked surprised by the question. 'You can't be serious,' she scorned.

'I can't?'

The other woman shook her head. 'Everyone knows Nick's background, it's never been any secret.'

'It has from me,' Rachel said casually, frightened of letting Suzy Freeman know just how much she wanted to know the answer to her next question. 'Tell me.'

'You really don't know?'

'No.'

'Oh, you walked right into it, didn't you?' Suzy scorned disbelievingly.

Her mouth twisted. 'So everyone keeps telling me.'

'You know, before I pitied you, now I really feel sorry for you. Nick must have verbally ripped you to shreds—and you don't even know why!'

'Are you going to tell me?' Rachel's voice was brittle.

'Why not?' Suzy shrugged. 'It's never been a secret. Shall we walk on, one of your cousins has just come out here with her boy-friend.'

'He's her husband, actually,' Rachel corrected, but she willingly moved out of earshot of the other couple.

'Your family believes in marrying young,' Suzy scorned. 'Were you frightened of getting left on the shelf, Rachel?'

Rachel ignored the jibe. 'We were talking about Nick,' she prompted.

'So we were.' Suzy sat down on the garden seat, waiting for Rachel to join her.

'Well?' Rachel prompted impatiently.

'Nick's life so far reads like a book,' Suzy derided. 'And it may or may not have a happy ending.' She gave Rachel a pointed look.

Colour tinged Rachel's cheeks. 'Go on.'

Suzy shrugged. 'Nick's mother wasn't married to his father. He was a very rich man, made no secret of the fact that Nick's mother had been no more than a one-night stand to him, although it became obvious she'd schemed to have his baby when she sued him for paternity. You're beginning to see the similarity?' she taunted.

'Yes.' Rachel felt sick.

'The case went on for months, with appeals and everything. When Nick's mother finally lost the case she did three things. She admitted that his father could be any one of a dozen men, she married the lawyer who'd been handling her case, and she put the child into an orphanage.'

'Nick . . .'

'Exactly,' Suzy said with satisfaction. 'She'd never really wanted him, although while the case was going on she seemed the model mother. He was three years old when she put him into care. It was in all the newspapers at the time, it was quite a scandal for thirty years ago. Then about ten years ago, just after Nick went professional, some reporter dug it all up again. Nick has never denied it.'

The whole thing must seem like a nightmare to Nick. No wonder he hated her, no wonder he was determined to have his child if there were one. And no wonder he had insisted on marrying her now—the idea of the same thing happening to his child that had happened to him must fill him with horror. And he could think her no better than his mother!

CHAPTER SIX

SUZY went on to tell Rachel about Nick's adoption when he was four, how his adoptive parents had had a child of their own a year later, of the love and happiness he had found in his new home.

But Rachel was only half listening, her thoughts mainly on the poor hurt little boy Nick had once been—which he still was inside? The scars of his early childhood were still inside him, had helped make him the man he was today, and that man could be harsh and cruel in his own way.

And no wonder! Oh, what a start in life for any child! It wasn't surprising that he insisted on being married to her.

She stood up abruptly. 'Shall we go back inside?'

Suzy also stood languidly to her feet. 'Of course. But remember, Nick belongs to me, has always belonged to me. And he will continue to do so, whether you stay married to him or not. I'd even bring up another woman's child for him,' she added slyly.

Rachel gave her a sharp look. 'Not my child you won't!'

Suzy gave her a half smile. 'We'll see. After all, the baby will be born legally now, there's no reason for you to stay around once it's been born.'

Except the obvious one—the baby was hers! Heavens, even she was starting to believe in this mythical baby now!

Nick was coming out of the lounge as the two women walked in from the garden, and his eyes narrowed as he looked at them both. 'I was just coming to look for you,' he told Rachel slowly.

Suzy Freeman gave a husky laugh. 'We were just having a woman-to-woman talk, darling.'

'Oh yes?'

'Yes,' she nodded. 'Your wife has just been telling me that she isn't in the least possessive.'

Hard blue eyes focused on Rachel. 'Has she now?'

Suzy reached up and kissed him lightly on the mouth. 'I'll see you Saturday, darling.'

'I'll look forward to it,' he drawled. Once the other girl had left his fingers bit painfully into Rachel's arm, pulling her to his side. 'Couldn't you wait until after the wedding to let everyone know you couldn't give a damn about me?' he ground out.

'Why should I wait?' she flashed, her pity for his childhood forgotten as he once again roused anger in her. 'When you've made no secret of it?'

'It's time we were leaving,' Nick said tightly. 'After all, I should make the most of having a wife, it may not be for long.'

'When I'm sure Miss Freeman will be glad to take over,' she snapped.

His mouth tightened. 'Let's go and say goodbye to your parents.'

'I have my suitcase upstairs——'

'Let's go and get it.' He marched her out of the room and up the stairs. 'Which room?' he demanded to know.

'Nick, please——'

'Which room, Rachel?' he rasped.

'This one,' she pushed the door open. 'But——'

He came inside, closing the door firmly behind them. 'Just what sort of conversation did you and Suzy have?' he scorned.

Her hands twisted nervously together. 'I—We—we talked about you—actually.'

'I'll bet you did,' he drawled. 'A nice cosy girlish chat,' he taunted.

'We didn't compare notes, if that's what you mean!' Rachel said fiercely. 'After all, I don't really have enough experience yet, do I?'

Nick's expression darkened ominously. 'Not yet, but you will,' he said grimly. 'And the sooner the better.' He picked up her suitcase and strode powerfully out of the room and down the stairs.

'You aren't leaving already?' Rachel's mother showed her disappointment as she came into the hallway to meet them.

The anger left Nick's face as he smiled at the other woman. 'I'm afraid so, Mrs James. After all, Rachel and I don't have a lot of time to be together before I leave for Boston.'

'Of course not,' her mother beamed at their desire to be alone. 'I'll just go and get Jim.'

Everyone else came out to say goodbye to them too, and the next few minutes were taken up in tearful goodbyes, even though they were only going to Nick's flat.

Rachel held back her tears as they drove through the busy streets, blinking rapidly, her throat aching from the suppressed tears. Her parents had looked so proud of her today, so pleased for her happiness.

'Cry if you want to,' Nick encouraged softly.

'I don't——'

'Stubbornness isn't going to change this situation. Cry if you want to!'

She did, deep racking sobs that shook her whole body. Her eyes were red and puffy by the time she had finished—not a pretty sight for a bride!

'Cheer up,' Nick taunted dryly. 'Your parents will still be around when this is over.'

'Your own parents—did you let them know we were getting married?' It hadn't occurred to her to ask before, but in the light of what Suzy had told her she felt curious to know what Nick's adoptive parents' reaction was to their marriage.

His expression was harsh. 'My parents died ten years ago, in an auto accident.'

Her heart contracted. Poor Nick! 'That's why you and Kay are so close,' she nodded understanding.

'We were always close,' he snapped. 'Always. She was the most beautiful baby I'd ever seen—nothing at all like Eve the day she was born,' he added mockingly.

'She's beautiful now,' Rachel defended. In just a week the baby had filled out, rounded, and considering she was only nine days old the transition was amazing. Nine days—could it really only be that short time since her life had changed so irrevocably? Somehow it seemed longer, much longer.

'Mm,' Nick nodded agreement. 'Do you like children? I never thought to ask before.'

'I love them!'

He gave her a frowning glance. 'No need to be so vehement, a simple yes or no would have sufficed.'

She had overreacted, she knew that, and yet she couldn't help herself; she hadn't wanted him to think her in the least like his mother. 'I just thought—in the circumstances——' she broke off awkwardly, knowing Nick wouldn't thank her for her pity.

'What circumstances?' he demanded grimly.

'Well, I—that I could be pregnant,' she invented. 'It would be as well if I liked children.'

'Yes,' he agreed distantly, accepting her explanation,

then he parked the car beneath the apartment building, getting her case out of the boot before guiding her over to the lift.

Mrs St Clare—she was Mrs St Clare, her life tightly bound to the man standing on the other side of the lift watching her so impersonally. No matter what happened, what the outcome of this marriage, for the moment she was Mrs Nick St Clare, married to a man who was a stranger to her—a man who knew her more intimately than any other human being.

The flat just the same, as impersonal as the man who lived in it, not a place one could call home. But it was her home now, hers and Nick's.

She looked at him nervously. 'I—Could I have a shower, please?' she asked shakily, she was still wearing the white dress and pillbox hat, feeling no need for a going-away outfit when she was only going a few minutes' drive down the road.

Nick shrugged, pouring himself a whisky from the decanter on the side. 'Go ahead.'

Rachel bit her bottom lip. 'Er—Which bedroom is mine?'

'*Our* bedroom is through here.' He led the way to the bedroom where he had made love to her, putting her suitcase on the ottoman at the bottom of the double bed, the blue patchwork quilt, matching curtains, and dark blue carpet showing it to be a masculine room, several male articles of clothing lying about the room. 'The bathroom is through here,' he opened a door to the left of the room, revealing a blue and white en-suite bathroom. 'Shower here, bath in the main bedroom. Take your pick,' he dismissed, turning to go back to his whisky.

Rachel watched him with clouded grey eyes.

'Shower, I think,' she said jerkily. 'I—I won't be long.'

'No hurry,' he shrugged, and closed the door behind him.

No hurry. No, there was no hurry about anything any more. Oh, what a few minutes of impetuosity could to to one's life!

And how Nick had suffered as a child! Rachel didn't think she would ever get over the shock of hearing how he had been treated, and she couldn't really blame him for not wanting the same fate for his own child. Not that she felt there was ever any danger of her being so cruel to her child, but Nick had no way of knowing that, he didn't know *her*. They were strangers locked in a marriage of convenience, and somehow they were going to have to live through it.

The shower refreshed her, her hair was brushed loosely down over her shoulders as she wrapped a towel about her before going back to the bedroom. She was just getting fresh clothing from her case when Nick walked into the room.

She had had no warning of his entrance, and she clutched her towel to her as she turned to face him. He had changed from his formal suit into a pair of snug-fitting denims and a black short-sleeved shirt, his hair still damp from where he had obviously made use of the main bathroom.

'I—I'm not dressed,' she told him nervously, her eyes huge in her pale face.

'I can see that,' he derided. 'Would you like to eat now or afterwards?'

Her eyes were wide in alarm. 'Afterwards . . .?'

'We're married now, Rachel,' he walked purposefully towards her, 'and I don't want to waste a minute of our time together before I leave on Saturday.'

She swallowed hard. 'I—I think I would rather have dinner now. I didn't eat much at the reception.'

'Too late,' he murmured. 'My appetite is aroused for you, not food. We can eat later.'

'Nick——'

'You're my wife, Rachel,' his eyes glittered down at her.

'But——'

'My wife . . .' His mouth came down on hers with a hunger he allowed full rein, holding nothing back as he manoeuvred her over to the bed, his gentle push knocking her off balance. He lay beside her as she fell against the patchwork quilt.

'Nick, dinner——'

His lips nuzzled her throat. 'There's only one thing I want from you as a wife, Rachel. And I can get that right here.' He looked down at her. 'Am I going to have to fight you?'

'Nick, please——'

'Am I?' he rasped.

'Yes!' her eyes flashed. 'Yes, you're going to have to fight me!' She pummelled his chest with her fists. 'All the way!' she vowed vehemently.

He gave a smile of satisfaction. 'I was hoping you would say that!'

Rachel looked at him with tear-filled eyes. 'Why?' she choked.

'Because tenderness isn't something I can give you. Every time I look at you I remember what you did, the way you schemed for this. I can give you desire, even pleasure, but I can't give you any of the love and tenderness a bride usually expects on her wedding night.'

'I don't want your love and tenderness—No!' she cried as he stripped the towel from her nakedness.

'No . . .' she groaned again as he pinned her arms at her side, shutting her eyes as he studied every inch of her naked body.

'Oh yes, Rachel,' he finally ground out. 'This is mine, bought and paid for by a marriage licence that isn't worth the paper it's printed on.'

Her eyes flew open, her breasts heaving in her anger. 'Take it, then!' she spat the words at him. 'Take it and be damned!'

'I was damned the day I met you,' Nick said harshly. 'But I will take your body, Rachel, however unwillingly it's given. Because it's mine, all mine, and it's the only thing I get from this marriage.'

She turned her face away, lying passively now. 'Take me, then,' she said dully. 'Just get it over with.'

His breath was inhaled angrily. 'It isn't going to be as easy as that, Rachel,' he warned softly. 'Not for you. I don't want a pretty doll in my bed, I want a flesh and blood woman, I want the response I got from you the other night.'

'I'll see you in hell first!'

'I've already been there,' he rasped. 'And I don't intend returning. You'll respond, Rachel, I can promise you that.'

'Promise away,' she challenged heatedly. 'I'll never respond to you—never!'

Oh, how traitorous the human body is! When she made the challenge she was so sure she could resist Nick, but she had reckoned without his expertise, his complete knowledge of the female body, of *her* body. Within minutes she was gasping her pleasure, was a willing recipient of his lovemaking, his wild caresses awakening a hunger within her that matched his own.

And even when their bodies shuddered to earth in mutual ecstasy Nick wasn't satisfied, raising her to the heights once more before they fell into a deep, satiated sleep.

When Rachel woke the flat was in darkness, and a glance at her luminous watch told her it was almost ten o'clock in the evening!

Nick lay heavily against her breasts; their sleep had been so deep neither of them seemed to have moved. But he was waking now, raising sleepy eyes to look at her, his arm about her waist wholly possessive.

'Is it morning?' he asked huskily.

'No.' She was almost afraid to speak, shy in front of him after the passion they had shared so deeply.

He blinked to clear the sleep from his brain. 'No?'

'It's still evening. Thursday evening.'

Nick sat up, pushing the hair from his eyes. 'Early or late?'

'Almost ten.' She avoided his gaze.

'Hungry?'

'Er—Not really.' She hadn't even thought about food!

'Nor me. Not for food anyway.'

Rachel could see the glow of his eyes as her vision became accustomed to the darkness. 'Nick . . .?'

'Decadent, isn't it?' he laughed softly, his hand caressing her breast. 'I want you again, Rachel.'

She wanted him too, wanted that closeness once again, that unity that even mutual ecstasy couldn't assuage.

They ate little the next day either; their conversation was almost non-existent, their lovemaking tempestuous and frequent. Rachel had never known such closeness to another person; neither of them needed to talk, their bodies said it all.

Until she woke late Saturday morning to find the bed beside her empty. Whenever she had woken the last two days Nick had been beside her, and she panicked to find him gone, and got hurriedly out of bed to look for him, caring nothing for her nakedness, the intimacies she had shared with Nick making a mockery of selfconsiousness. She didn't think she would ever be shy with him again.

He wasn't in the bathroom, and he wasn't in the kitchen either, in fact he wasn't anywhere in the flat! Rachel was really beginning to panic when she saw the message on the pad beside the telephone, the handwriting Nick's: 'If you need me—urgently!—call this number', and he had listed a telephone number beneath.

He had gone to Boston! After two days of constant lovemaking, of feeling an incredible oneness with him, Nick had gone to the tournament in Boston without even saying goodbye to her!

Her parents invited her over for the day on Sunday, realising she would be lonely in Nick's absence. How lonely they would never know! Rachel had spent all day yesterday in the flat waiting for Nick to call her, sure that he would let her know he had arrived safely. There had been no call.

Pride kept her from calling the number he had left her, although she longed just to hear the sound of his voice. But the addition of the word urgent had been more than clear; he didn't want to hear from her unless she was ill or dying—or unless she knew she wasn't expecting his child!

Her parents noticed her listless behaviour, and her mother remarked on it after lunch. 'Maybe you should have gone with Nick,' she said gently. 'Just this once.'

'My exams——'

'I know, dear,' her mother nodded, 'but you look so miserable.'

'I'll get over it,' Rachel sighed. 'And he'll be back in two weeks.'

'But only for a week. Still, at least next time you'll be able to go with him.'

Rachel looked down at her hands. She and Nick had never discussed her going with him, but if she had to watch him and Suzy Freeman together then she would rather stay here. 'I don't know if Nick wants that. He—he's very busy, and he doesn't like the distraction.'

'Oh, but surely——'

'Maybe later on, Mum,' she said awkwardly.

'But——'

'Leave them alone, Dorothy,' her father interrupted sternly. 'They can arrange their own lives.'

'But, Jim, I was only——'

'Leave it, Dorothy,' he warned. 'Or Nick will think he has an interfering mother-in-law,' he added teasingly.

'I'm only concerned for Rachel,' she said indignantly. 'It isn't natural for a bride to be on her own two days after the wedding.'

He shrugged. 'Worse things happened during the war. And at least they can telephone each other, isn't that right, Rachel?' he eyed her questioningly.

'Yes, Dad,' she hurriedly agreed with him.

Nevertheless, her father spoke to her alone before she left, while her mother was out in the kitchen.

'Is everything—all right, Rachel?' asked concernedly.

'Of course.' Her voice was brittle.

A ruddy hue coloured his cheeks. 'Your mother and I never talked to you about—well, about being married,' he swallowed awkwardly, looking very uncomfortable. 'By the time we thought we should talk to you about it they were teaching it to you at school.

And quite frankly, Nick appeared to me the sort of man who would know how to treat an inexperienced bride.'

Rachel was blushing too by this time. As her father said, sex was something that had never been discussed between them before. 'He did,' she said huskily.

Her father nodded, as if he had never doubted it. 'He's a good man. You are happy with him?'

'Yes, Dad,' she laughingly kissed him on the cheek. 'I'm just missing him, that's all.'

'Okay, pet,' he smiled. 'And you come and see us any time you like, as often as you like. To tell you the truth, it's a bit quiet around here without you. Your mother misses you dreadfully.'

'Maybe you should have another baby,' she teased.

'At our age!' he scoffed. 'No, we're quite happy to wait for our grandchildren to come along.'

That might not be too far in the future, if her father did but know it!

The next two weeks dragged by, with no word from Nick, not even a postcard telling her when he would be back. Her time was ably filled that first week, in the day at last, the exams taking up most of her time. But the second week college came to an end, and she found time really dragging, the occasional afternoon shopping with Hilary or her mother being her only outings.

Not that she ever bought anything! She might be Nick's wife, living in his home, but he had made no arrangements for her to receive any money to feed or clothe herself. She had a small amount of money saved, not much, having been at school most of her life, but she used that to buy food and pay the bills.

As far as she knew Nick was due back some time on Monday, so she could use the last of her savings to get food in for his return.

Although it was only nine o'clock on Sunday evening, she was already in bed when she heard the key in the lock. Nick! It had to be Nick.

She scrambled out of bed, forgetting her hurt at his silence of the past two weeks, and ran out into the hallway, uncaring of the scantiness of her short nightgown as she stared hungrily at Nick. He looked tired, pale beneath his tan, with lines of weariness about his eyes.

He hadn't seen her yet, and he dropped his suitcase on the floor, discarding his black leather jerkin before turning. He halted in his tracks. 'Rachel . . .!' he breathed softly, as if surprised to see her there.

Rachel licked her lips nervously, unsure of how to greet him. 'Hello,' she finally answered inadequately.

He quirked a mocking eyebrow. 'No welcome home from my wife?'

'Of course,' she nodded jerkily, coming forward to kiss him lightly on the cheek. 'Welcome home.'

'Can't you do better than that?' he taunted.

Anger started to burn within her. After two weeks of not even so much as a telephone call he calmly walked back in here and expected a hero's welcome! 'Yes, I can do better,' she said tightly, and moved out of his arms. 'Were they hard tournaments? Did you have to play hard to win in Boston? Congratulations on the win, by the way. You must be exhausted. Why don't you go into the lounge and I'll bring you a cup of coffee.'

Nick looked exasperated by her behaviour. 'Rachel, what the hell are you babbling about?'

She gave him a cool look. 'I'm not babbling, I'm acting as a wife should. We're supposed to ask the husband about his work when he gets home.

Admittedly he hasn't usually been away for two weeks, but——'

'Rachel, will you shut up,' he growled. 'Please!'

She gave him a startled look. 'P-please?'

'Yes,' he grimaced. 'Shut up and let me kiss you.'

Rachel was determined to be withdrawn, not to respond, but as on their wedding day she was powerless to resist him. Tonight his desire was ceaseless, seeming to draw the very soul from her before he took them both over the edge into ecstasy.

When Rachel woke she was once again alone, only this time she could hear noises in the flat, telling her that Nick was still here. She hugged herself pleasurably as she thought of the week they would have together this time.

Nick came back into the room wearing a towelling robe, scowling heavily. 'There's no food in the fridge.'

Hot colour flooded her cheeks. 'I—I was going to go shopping tomorrow,' she explained lamely.

'But there's no food now, Rachel!'

'No,' she acknowledged huskily.

His eyes narrowed. 'Why isn't there?'

She swallowed hard. 'I—because—well——'

'Well?' he prompted.

Rachel propped herself up on her elbows, not noticing how provocative her naked breasts appeared to her husband. 'You didn't leave me any money for food,' she snapped. 'In fact, you didn't leave me any money for anything. The man downstairs on the desk brought back some cleaning of yours, and the milkman wanted paying. I had no idea how much you normally paid for those things, so I—I gave them their money.'

'You borrowed from your parents?' he said grimly.

'Certainly not!' She would never admit such a thing to her parents. 'I used my savings.'

'But you ran out?'

'Yes,' she nodded awkwardly.

'When?'

'Well, I still have a few pounds, but I was going to use that to get some food in the morning, so that we could have a nice meal when you got back.'

'When did you stop eating, Rachel?'

'I——'

'When?' he demanded harshly.

She shrugged. 'I haven't stopped eating, I've just cut down.'

'I can see that,' he snapped tautly. 'I could *feel* that. Why didn't you call me, Rachel? I left you the number where I could be reached.'

'In an emergency!' Her eyes were stormy.

'And you didn't think your starving to death was an emergency?' he thundered.

'I'm not starving——'

'Aren't you?' His gaze raked over her critically. 'God, you were thin enough before, now you're skeletal!'

'I'm slim——'

'You're all skin and bone!'

'And whose fault is that? I'm sorry,' she cried as he blanched. 'I'm sorry, Nick. I didn't mean that.'

'Why not?—it's the truth,' he said grimly. 'First thing tomorrow morning I'm going out to buy food, then when you've eaten enough to get your strength back——'

'I'm sorry if my performance wasn't good enough,' she choked, tears in her eyes.

'You were exquisite—as usual,' Nick ground out, and came to sit on the side of the bed, his gaze searching as it roamed slowly over her flushed face. 'Don't cry, Rachel.'

The one sure way to guarantee that someone cries is to tell them not to! Rachel buried her face in her hands as the tears cascaded down her cheeks.

Nick pulled her gently against him. 'I'm sorry, Rachel,' he murmured into her silky hair. 'I never gave money a thought.'

She gave him a watery smile. 'Rich people seldom do.'

'No,' he agreed ruefully. 'Anyway, I'm sorry. And straight after breakfast I'm taking you to the bank to arrange a joint account.' He smoothed her hair back from her face, drying her tears. 'I wish you had called me, Rachel.'

'I thought you wouldn't want me to bother you,' she revealed shyly.

His expression darkened, his hands gently caressing her shoulders. 'Never think that again,' he said huskily, and his mouth lowered to one pert nipple. 'God, I missed you,' he groaned against her heated flesh.

'Nick . . .?'

'I missed you!' He silenced her surprised gasp very effectively with his mouth on hers.

Rachel awoke next morning to the mouthwatering smell of bacon and eggs and fresh coffee, and she stretched languidly in the bed just as Nick came into the bedroom carrying a tray. He placed the bedtable across her legs, revealing bacon, eggs, and tomatoes, lots of toast, a bowl of marmalade, and a steaming pot of coffee.

She looked up at him gratefully. 'You shouldn't have done this. I could have cooked breakfast.'

He sat down on the side of the bed as she began to eat. 'Not without the food. I went out this morning and got some groceries.'

Her eyes widened. 'You must have been up early!'

'Hmm,' he agreed ruefully. 'My timing is all out from the flight. I've already eaten,' he refused as she offered him the toast. 'Once you've finished that we'll go out.'

It felt strange to hear the bank manager calling her Mrs St Clare; only the commissionaire to the apartments, and the milkman, had called her by that name so far, the latter somewhat sceptically, she had thought. But with Nick introducing her as his wife no one dared doubt it.

As there had only been a week left of college she hadn't informed anyone there, except Hilary, of course, of her married status. After all, by the time she returned in September it could all be over!

Nick took her out for lunch, and the two of them talked over the matches he had played while he had been away. He had won the tournament in Boston, but the one in Washington he had been knocked out of during the quarter-finals.

He shrugged. 'You win some, you lose some.'

'Do you win many?' Rachel asked interestedly, finding that tennis was a subject they could talk about without arguing.

'A few,' he answered consideringly. 'Although it gets harder all the time. Apart from the fact that you had no money, were you all right while I was away?' he asked intently.

Delicate colour heightened her cheeks. 'I don't know anything yet, if that's what you mean.'

For a moment Nick looked startled. 'No, that isn't what I meant,' he rasped.

'Oh!' Rachel looked confused.

'How did your exams go?' he asked.

'Er—fine.' She was totally thrown by his interest, especially after the argument they had had when she had decided to stay in England to take the exams.

Nick quirked an eyebrow. 'Think you passed?'

'I hope so.'

'You won't be able to carry on with college if you're pregnant, you know.'

'I do know,' she nodded. 'But just this one year has been helpful.'

'What did you intend doing with the subject?'

Rachel shrugged. 'Maybe starting my own business one day. If I ever got enough money,' she joked.

Nick sipped the chilled white wine which was all he had drunk with his meal. 'If this doesn't work out I could——'

'No!' she refused sharply, knowing exactly what he was going to say.

'No?'

She shook her head. 'If it doesn't work out I'll leave this marriage the same way I came into it, with nothing.'

Nick's mouth twisted. 'You say that now . . .'

Rachel paled, the enjoyable morning they had spent together suddenly fading away. 'I feel sorry for you,' she scorned, the image of a hurt little boy she had been carrying around with her all morning disappearing in the face of his derision. He might have suffered as a young child, but his adoptive parents had shown him plenty of love, and Kay adored him, and he had no reason for bitterness now. 'You mistrust everyone!'

He stood up. 'Only clever little girls like you, my dear,' he drawled. 'I have to leave you now——'

'You do?' She hoped her disappointment wasn't too obvious.

It appeared not; Nick looked at his wrist-watch. 'I have a practice session this afternoon.'

'But we haven't had a honeymoon yet!'

His eyes mocked her. 'We have, but I'll remind you of it later. I practise for a couple of hours every day, even when I'm not playing. I have to.'

'And will Miss Freeman be at this—practice session?' she asked coolly.

Nick shrugged. 'She usually looks in.'

'I see.'

'I doubt it,' he derided. 'I'll be home in time for dinner.'

She childishly told herself she didn't care if he never came back, but she knew it wasn't true. Nevertheless, her coolness towards him lasted through dinner, a coolness Nick treated with amusement. The moment they got to bed it became obvious why, as her body melted into his in complete surrender.

Their life fell into a pattern over the next few days. Their mornings were spent together—more often than not in bed; Nick spent the afternoon at the court, and then their evenings were spent together too. It was a tranquil and satisfying existence, and Rachel dreaded the time he would go away again.

They had dinner with her parents one evening, and she could tell that they really liked her husband. And Nick seemed to like them too; his voice was genuinely warm and friendly when he spoke to them.

All too soon Saturday came around again. Nick's flight was another early morning one. He had made no mention of taking Rachel with him, and she had been afraid of rejection if she suggested it.

'I want to come to the airport with you in the morning,' she told Nick as they lay in bed together on Friday night.

He grimaced. 'I don't like goodbyes, I never have.'

'I noticed,' she said dryly.

His mouth quirked mockingly. 'I know a much

better way of saying goodbye than with words.'

'Nick——'

'You'll like this goodbye, Rachel,' he murmured, his body covering hers.

When she woke in the morning she was once more alone, only the smell of Nick's aftershave lingering on the pillow next to her and his hastily discarded robe telling her the last week hadn't been a dream.

Or a nightmare! She had at last realised what that threatening shadow was. She had fallen in love with her own husband, loved him deeply; she only felt truly alive when she was with him!

She had known she felt strongly about him, known it wasn't just physical attraction as she kept telling herself it was, but that she would come to love him more than life itself she had never guessed.

CHAPTER SEVEN

THE next week dragged by even slower than the last time Nick had been away, and Rachel's loss was all the more acute because of her accepted love for him. From the moment she had met him, even when she had thought him to be Kay's husband or live-in lover, she had been totally aware of him. Her love had grown without her even being aware of it, and it came as something of a shock to realise how dependent she was on him, emotionally.

That first week without him was an agony of loneliness, and she often woke during the night clutching the pillow in her arms. It was then that she cried, then that she knew when this marriage ended she would be devastated.

When Kay invited her round to dinner on the Saturday she was pleased to accept; she was tired of her own company. As last time, Nick had made no effort to call her, only this time the silence was worse.

But being with Kay and Richard Lennox wasn't a good idea either. The normality of their marriage made a mockery of her own; the only level she and Nick communicated on was a physical one. But the Lennoxes' marriage was one of deep love and friendship, neither of which she and Nick had.

'It really is too bad of my brother,' Kay admonished, 'going off and leaving you like this all the time.'

Rachel shrugged, 'He has to play.' They had finished dinner and were now in the lounge, Eve snugly tucked up in her cot upstairs.

'He doesn't, but that's beside the point. He could have taken you with him this time.'

'Kay!'

'I know,' Kay acknowledged her husband's warning, 'I said I wouldn't interfere. But I really think Nick should have taken Rachel with him, she's finished college now.'

'I'd just be in the way——'

'Nonsense!' Kay dismissed. 'Suzy travels everywhere with Sam and Nick, and she doesn't get in the way.'

'I'm sure she doesn't,' Rachel agreed jerkily, standing up. 'I think I'd better go now. It's late, and——'

'It's only nine-thirty,' her sister-in-law frowned.

'I know, but I—I really have to go.'

Kay frowned, joining her at the door. 'Hey, was it anything I said? I mean, if it was, I'm sorry.'

Rachel shook her head. 'It was nothing, really. I just—Nick may call,' she invented desperately.

'Ah, now I understand,' Kay nodded, smiling. 'Well, give him my love.'

'Can I drive you home?' Richard offered.

'No, thanks,' Rachel smiled; she liked Kay's husband immensely. 'I have the car with me.'

Nick had offered her the keys to his car, but only being a newly qualified driver she had been petrified of the monster and had refused, so Nick had instantly gone out and bought her a Mini—much to her delighted surprise.

'I'll call you,' Kay told her warmly, and Rachel knew that she would. Kay was a nice woman, a thoughtful friend.

The flat seemed lonelier than ever on her return from the warmth and spontaneous love that flowed in the Lennox household, and she wandered aimlessly from room to room. When the telephone rang she jumped nervously, then picked up the receiver. It was probably her parents, they rang most evenings.

'Rachel?'

Nick's husky tones had her sitting upright in the chair. 'Nick?' she exclaimed excitedly.

'Who else were you expecting to call you?'

She bristled at his suspicious tone. 'No one. But then I wasn't expecting a call from you either,' she snapped, her happiness at hearing from him evaporating.

'Enjoying yourself?' he taunted.

'Oh yes,' her voice was brittle, 'I'm going out having fun every night.'

'Who with?' he asked sharply.

'Surely you don't expect me to list them?' she scorned.

'Rachel——'

'Oh, for goodness' sake, Nick, don't be so ridiculous! I've been in every night——'

'You were out tonight. I called earlier and got no reply.'

'I was at your sister's. I think she felt sorry for me.'

'Something I'm sure you nurture,' he said nastily.

'Oh yes,' she derided, 'I tell her how cruel you are to me—when I see you. How I'm your damned sex-slave!' She was really angry now. 'How dare you call me up like this and insult me? What did you call for anyway?' she added moodily.

'To ask you to join me in Canada,' he told her quietly.

'*What?*'

'I'm lonely, I'd like you here with me.'

Rachel blinked, swallowing hard, completely speechless. *He* was lonely? How did he think she felt!

'Rachel?'

She licked her lips nervously. 'I don't know what to say.'

'You could try yes,' Nick taunted softly.

'I——'

'Nick darling, are you ready for dinner yet?'

The sound of Suzy Freeman's husky voice came clearly over the telephone! 'So you're lonely, are you, Nick?' Rachel snapped. 'Well, maybe I should go out and find myself some loneliness like that!' She slammed the receiver down, then ran into her bedroom to bury her head beneath the pillow as she sobbed, the sound of the telephone ringing muffled as she held the pillow tightly over her ears.

She must have finally fallen asleep that way, for she woke in the morning to find she was still fully dressed, the pillow still over her head. Nick had been very persistent; the telephone had rung again and again—until presumably he had gone off to dinner with Suzy Freeman!

How dared he ask her to join him when Suzy Freeman was in the room with him? More to the point, why bother with her when the other woman was more than willing to occupy her place in his bed?

She wouldn't allow herself to dwell on this further hurt, and spent the day with her parents, doing her best to forget she even had a husband.

The telephone was once again ringing when she got in at ten o'clock, and she knew it had to be Nick. She considered ignoring it again, but knew from experience that he would just keep ringing and ringing.

'Yes?' she snapped into the receiver.

'Rachel?' The voice on the line was definitely female!

'Er—yes.' She frowned. She had been so sure it was going to be Nick, and was taken aback that it wasn't.

'Suzy Freeman here, Rachel,' she was informed.

She instantly stiffened. 'Yes?'

'You really weren't very sensible yesterday, Rachel,' the other girl taunted.

'I wasn't?' she evaded.

'No,' Suzy gave a throaty laugh. 'Nick hates jealousy. I warned you you wouldn't hold on to him for long. Physical attraction isn't enough, you know.'

'It was enough for Nick to ask me to join him in Canada!' Rachel snapped—and then wished she hadn't. She hated letting this girl know she disturbed her— even if she did.

'Nick hates to sleep alone,' Suzy drawled.

Rachel swallowed hard. 'You mean——'

'I mean that Nick loves the one he's with, and as you refused to join him . . . Well, I'm sure you understand what I mean,' Suzy said coyly.

She understood only too well, and she was sickened by the thought of Nick and Suzy together. 'Did you call me just to let me know that you slept with my husband last night?' she asked stiffly.

'No,' Suzy laughed. 'Although I did think you should know about it.'

'Thank you!'

'My pleasure—and I mean that literally,' the other woman purred. 'Nick is such a considerate lover, isn't he?'

'Yes,' Rachel agreed dully.

'Anyway, enough of that,' Suzy said briskly. 'I'm sure you're as familiar with Nick's prowess in bed as I am. I'm calling on his behalf actually.'

'Really?' Rachel scorned. 'Did he want me to know the two of you slept together too?'

'I'm sure he wouldn't deny it if you asked him.'

'I have no intention of asking him anything,' Rachel snapped.

'Please yourself,' she could hear the shrug in Suzy's voice. 'Nick's practising right now. He called your earlier, but didn't get an answer.'

'I've been out all day.'

'Obviously,' Suzy said dryly. 'Nick didn't like it.'

'Shame!'

'I wouldn't get clever with him, Rachel. He can be—well, he has a temper.'

'I'll bear that in mind!'

'Rachel—Oh, never mind, it's your funeral. The sooner the two of you split up the better I'll like it.'

'So I gathered.'

'Okay, as long as we know where we stand. Nick still wants you to come out here.'

Rachel frowned. 'Couldn't you convince him otherwise?' she taunted.

'I tried. But Nick is afraid that the news of your marriage may leak out to the press. It wouldn't look very good for his image if it were known he'd left you in England only a month after the wedding.'

In that moment Rachel truly hated Nick. He hadn't wanted her with him at all; he just didn't want any adverse publicity.

'And talking of months,' Suzy continued, 'Nick wondered if you knew anything yet?' she mocked.

'If I did I wouldn't tell my husband's mistress!' And Rachel slammed the telephone down.

The truth of the matter was she still wasn't sure of her condition one way or the other. With all that had happened to her the last few weeks her body had gone haywire.

Nick telephoned her himself later in the evening. 'Suzy says you won't come out to Canada,' he said tersely.

'No.' She clutched the receiver. She had not expected to hear from him once Suzy had told him of their conversation.

'Why the hell not?'

'I'm sure Suzy told you my reasons.' She was at once on the defensive.

'She did,' he confirmed. 'But I want you out here '

'She told me that too, and the reason why.'

'And?'

'I'm still not coming.' She didn't give a damn about adverse publicity.

'Rachel——'

'I'm not interested, Nick.' She was too hurt by the fact that his interest should only be in what the press had to say. Oh, she had no doubt that once she was there he would want her to share his bed, but it would all really be for show. Nick was only thinking of his image. That was probably also part of the reason he had married her in the first place. No doubt his childhood had influenced his decision, but more controversial publicity for someone as much in the public eye as he was could have something to do with it too.

He gave an angry sigh. 'I need you out here.'

'And I'm quite happy where I am.'

'You're my wife——'

'And you're my husband!' she reminded him tightly.

'What's that supposed to mean?'

'Work it out, Nick. Goodnight.'

'Rachel——'

'Goodnight!'

Tonight he didn't bother to call her back, and her sleep was restless as she accepted that the gulf between her and Nick was widening.

As the time neared for him to come home her ner-

vousness about facing him again increased. It was one
thing to defy him over the telephone, quite another to
accept his wrath face to face.

There was a girl waiting outside the flat when she
arrived home from shopping one evening.

'Yes?' Rachel frowned her puzzlement, sure that she
didn't know the girl.

'Mrs St Clare?'

'Yes.' Her frown deepened, and she tried to balance
her shopping while she unlocked the door.

'Here, let me.' The girl took one of the shopping
bags out of her hand.

'Thanks,' Rachel gave a grateful smile, and led the
way inside, putting the shopping in the kitchen.

'You've been busy.' The other girl put the bag she
had been carrying on the worktop beside the others.

'Yes.' Rachel ran her hands nervously down her
denim-clad thighs. 'Er—Nick's away right now.' It
followed that if she didn't know this girl then she must
be a friend of Nick's!

'Yes, I know,' the girl nodded.

Oh God, not another of Nick's women come to warn
her off! This girl looked three or four years older than
her, still a little young for Nick, but that didn't rule
out the possibility of her being another one of his girl-
friends. If Nick wanted someone badly enough then he
wasn't likely to let a thing like age bother him. It hadn't
with her.

'He won't be back until Sunday,' she said.

'I know,' the girl nodded again.

'Oh.' Rachel chewed on her bottom lip. 'Then I
don't see—er——' she shook her head in puzzlement.
'I don't think I can help you.'

The girl gave an embarrassed laugh. 'I'm sorry—
I'm new at this sort of thing. I should have introduced

myself. My name is Anna Hill, and I work for the *Morning News*, and——'

'You're a reporter?' Rachel gasped in dismay.

'Afraid so,' Anna Hill nodded ruefully.

'Oh dear!'

'Everyone reacts the same way,' the other girl sighed.

Rachel blushed. 'It's nothing personal.'

'Oh, I know that,' Anna Hill laughed.

Rachel clutched her hands together in front of her. 'I really don't see how I can help you.' She looked at the girl with anxious grey eyes.

'You *are* Mrs St Clare, Mrs *Nick* St Clare?'

'Er—yes.' She frowned. 'Nothing has happened to Nick, has it?' Panic clutched at her heart.

Anna Hill shrugged. 'Not unless you call getting knocked out of the Canadian Open something "happening" to him.'

'Oh no!' Rachel groaned.

' 'Fraid so,' the other girl nodded. 'We had information at the paper that he'd recently married——'

'Who from?' Rachel interrupted sharply.

Anna Hill shrugged. 'I have no idea. My editor came to me with the story, I'm just following it up.'

'I see.'

'I hope so,' the girl grimaced. 'I hate these sort of stories.'

'These sort?' Rachel queried tentatively.

'Well, since you married a few weeks ago your husband has won one tournament, hasn't played at all, or has been knocked out in the early stages. I'm supposed to find out if you think your marriage has affected his play.'

Rachel drew in a controlling breath. 'Obviously someone thinks it has,' she said tightly.

'Not me. When I saw him play at Wimbledon——'

'We weren't married then.'

'Oh. No, you weren't, were you? I thought he should have won.'

'Yes.'

'You would rather I weren't here, wouldn't you?' Anna Hill sighed.

'I——'

'It's all right,' the other girl smiled. 'I'm getting used to it. It used to upset me a lot at first, but I think I'm getting hardened to it.'

Rachel couldn't help liking Anna Hill—although she didn't like the reason she was here at all. Nick was a well-known tennis personality, and perhaps they had been lucky to evade publicity over their marriage this long, but she couldn't say she liked this sudden interest; it embarrassed and unnerved her.

'Would you object to the interview?' Anna Hill prompted gently.

'I—I think that would depend on the questions you want to ask,' Rachel decided.

,'Yes. But I think I should warn you that if I don't get the story some other newspaper is going to pick it up. And although I say it myself, I think I could handle it better than a lot of them.'

Rachel sighed and turned away. She had seen some of the sensationalism printed in the newspapers nowadays, and if it was true that Nick had once again been eliminated from a tournament, the important Canadian Open, then the story of their recent marriage could make very lurid reading. Anna Hill seemed a very sensitive girl, and she was easy to talk to.

She turned back to the other girl. 'Could I read the story before it was submitted?'

'You learn fast!' Anna grinned.

'I think I may have to,' Rachel said dryly.

'Yes,' Anna agreed ruefully. 'But I never put in anything that isn't approved by the person I'm writing about—less chance of a libel suit that way. It may be exciting to get an exclusive, but it isn't so exciting if your subject takes some exception to what you've written.'

'Would you like some coffee?' Rachel offered.

'I'd love some,' Anna accepted eagerly.

After days of being alone it was good to have company, although perhaps a reporter wasn't the best person in the world to open your heart up to! Rachel only gave Anna the bare facts of her meeting with Nick through Kay, realising as she told it how romantic it sounded.

'Love at first sight,' Anna said dreamily.

'Not quite—maybe second sight,' Rachel added at the other girl's disappointment.

'You're so lucky!'

Nick obviously had another eager female fan here. 'Very,' she agreed abruptly, feeling jealous in spite of herself.

'No wonder Nick—Mr St Clare——'

'Nick,' Rachel accepted.

'Well, no wonder he's off his game. He must really be missing you.'

'Yes.' She sounded distant now.

'Why aren't you in Canada with him?'

'Well, he did ask me to go,' Rachel said truthfully, 'but I'd just be a distraction to him.'

'Mm, it's a difficult decision to make. You're a distraction if you're there, and a distraction if you aren't there.'

'Yes.'

'You must really miss him too.'

'Yes,' she answered truthfully.

'Right—well, I think I have enough to be going on with.' Anna Hill stood up, checking her notes.

Once the other girl had gone Rachel wondered if she had told her too much. It had only been the truth, but without the fact of Nick making love to her and then forcing her to marry him it came out as a rather romantic story.

As the evening passed and she heard nothing back from Anna her worry deepened. She even called the newspaper once, only to be told Anna was out covering a story. She left her name with a message for the girl to call her the minute she got back, whatever time it happened to be.

It was just after eleven when the doorbell rang, and she rushed to answer it. It was Anna Hill.

'Sorry it's so late,' she said breathlessly, 'but I was out covering a fire——'

'Was anyone hurt?'

'No, thank God.'

'Come in.' Rachel held the door open.

'I'm a bit smoky——'

'It doesn't matter,' Rachel dismissed, leading the way to the lounge.

Anna looked guilty as she followed her. 'I have a confession to make . . .'

Rachel stiffened. 'Yes?'

'I'm so sorry—There just wasn't time, you see, not with the fire and everything.' She gave Rachel a pleading look.

Rachel closed her eyes for a moment, pale as she looked at Anna. 'You've submitted the story, haven't you?' she guessed tautly.

'I didn't, my editor did. I was called out to this fire, and I'd left your story on my desk. My editor saw it and took it.'

Rachel bit her lip. 'Can I see it now?'

'Of course.' Anna looked through her handbag. 'I brought you one of the first run-offs. The photograph came out well, didn't it?' She looked over Rachel's shoulder as she read the article.

Rachel had given Anna one of the photographs of the wedding, and even if she did say so herself it was a good one, of both of them. Somehow they had been looking at each other, Nick indulgently so, she with a dreamy look in her eyes.

As she read the article her heart sank. It was full of quotes from her, so obviously given at an interview, and in print the story looked ridiculously romantic, almost like a fairytale.

'You don't like it,' Anna sighed at her silence.

It wasn't that she didn't like it, she just didn't think Nick would. But there wasn't a word of a lie in the whole article, and as she had thought it would be, it was written with sensitivity, even if Anna had also introduced an enjoyment of the romantic.

'I don't *not* like it——'

'Did I go too far?' Anna asked worriedly.

'Well . . .'

'I did,' she grimaced. 'I knew it should have been checked with you first.'

'It doesn't matter.' Rachel handed the newsheet back to Anna. 'It's done now.'

'I'm really sorry you don't like it.'

'Don't worry about it,' Rachel assured the other girl. 'I'm not going to.'

That must have been the biggest lie of the century! She lay awake all night wondering what Nick was going to say when—if, he saw the article. As he was in

Canada there was always the chance that he just might not hear about it.

But everyone else did! Her mother passed on messages of good wishes from friends she hadn't heard from for years. But she heard nothing from Nick, something she was grateful for. By tomorrow they would, quite literally, be yesterday's news, and with luck would hear no more about it.

This time she took no chances on Nick arriving home early, and stocked the fridge up on Friday with all the foods he liked.

But she needn't have bothered. Nick didn't arrive home Friday, or on the Saturday as he had said he would. By late Sunday evening Rachel was getting really worried, but she knew that if she started checking up on Nick, and there was no need for alarm, he would be furious with her.

She was sitting in the lounge at nine-thirty when she heard the key in the lock. It had to be Nick, and yet pride kept her seated. He had made no effort to call her and let her know he would be late, or the reason for it, and as far as she was concerned he had some explaining to do.

She heard him go to the bedroom, and then his firm tread coming in this direction, and her interest was suddenly intent on the play on the television that seconds ago she hadn't even realised was on.

Nick didn't say a word, but moved to the array of drinks on the sideboard to pour himself a glass of whisky. He drank the contents of the glass with one swallow, refilling it to leave the room. A couple of seconds later she heard the sound of the shower being run.

He had looked so tired, very grey and drawn, thinner in the face too. And in the face of his exhaustion her sulky behaviour suddenly seemed childish. Once he had showered she would get him some dinner and perhaps they could sit and talk for a while.

But not for too long! One thing his being away from her this time had done was to make her want him quite shamelessly. Only in bed could they truly communicate, and she wanted that closeness with him again as soon as possible.

She waited in vain for him to return to the lounge, finally getting up to investigate. The bedroom was in darkness, a lone figure stretched out beneath the bedclothes, the even tenor of his breathing telling her that Nick was already asleep.

Rachel quietly left the room and went back to the lounge, her disappointment acute. It was the first time since their wedding, on the nights that Nick had been home, that he hadn't wanted to make love to her. Of course he was tired from the flight, but he had been tired other nights, and it hadn't stopped him wanting her then.

He didn't even stir as she got into bed beside him a short time later; his sleep seemed deeply drugged, her own tossings and turnings not seeming to bother him at all.

When she woke in the morning he was gone, only the indent of his head on the pillow beside her telling her that he had been beside her at all. The case he usually took away with him was still in the wardrobe, so he hadn't gone on another tournament without telling her.

He arrived back at the flat at lunchtime, and went briefly into the bedroom to collect the bag he usually took on practice sessions before leaving again.

Rachel chewed worriedly on her bottom lip, her nerves frayed to breaking point. Maybe he was still angry about their last telephone conversation? Or maybe he had seen the newspaper after all?

She was in the kitchen preparing dinner when he arrived home shortly before seven, and looked up anxiously as he came to stand in the doorway.

'Don't get any dinner for me,' he told her abruptly.

'Oh, but——'

'I'm going out again.' He moved in the direction of the bedroom.

'Nick——'

'Yes?' he snapped.

'I—But I've made your favourite meal,' she said desperately. 'Steak in wine sauce.'

'Maybe it will heat up for tomorrow,' he dismissed callously.

Rachel had spent hours preparing the sauce and steak as he liked it, had even gone to the trouble of making him an apple pie for dessert. 'It will be ruined,' she told him dully.

'Then throw it away.'

'Nick——'

He gave an impatient sigh. 'What is it now?'

She blinked back her tears. 'Nothing. I'm sorry I troubled you.' She went back to the kitchen and threw the food away, having no appetite for it herself.

'Goodbye!' he called out a few minutes later, the flat door banging shut behind him.

'Oh, but——' By the time she had got into the hall-way he had already gone.

But where had he gone? He hadn't wanted dinner, so obviously he was going to have it out, but who with? She didn't really need two guesses at the answer to that. Suzy Freeman was getting her wish, and a lot sooner than anticipated!

This time Rachel was the one to fall asleep, her sleepless night from the night before taking its toll. The next morning was a repeat of the one before, rumpled sheets and pillow telling her that Nick had slept beside her, although she had no idea what time he had arrived home.

Well, they couldn't go on like this. They hadn't spoken more than half a dozen words to each other in the whole of the time he had been back.

But it seemed they *could* go on like that, and for the next two days she saw even less of Nick—if that were possible.

By the Friday evening she had had enough of it; she couldn't stand the way things were between them any longer. Instead of going to bed and falling asleep before Nick got home as she usually did, she waited up for him. It was almost one o'clock in the morning when he got home, and his eyes narrowed on her as she came out to meet him.

'What the hell are you still doing up?' he rasped. He had been drinking—heavily, by the way he lurched into the lounge.

'Waiting for you,' Rachel stated the obvious.

His mouth turned back contemptuously. 'Well, I'm sorry, Rachel, but I'm not in the mood to give you what you want tonight.'

She flushed at the insult. 'Nor any other night lately,' she muttered before she could stop herself.

'Missing it, are you, Rachel?' he sneered.

'Not at all——'

'Liar,' he scorned, his tie loosened at his throat, the top two buttons of his shirt undone. 'The way you cling to me in the night tells me otherwise.'

Colour flooded her cheeks. 'I didn't know . . .'

'No,' he taunted, 'you do it instinctively.'

'Nick, what's wrong?' Her expression was pained, appealing.

'Wrong?' he repeated sharply, pouring himself a glass of whisky.

She frowned worriedly as he drank it down as if it were water. 'Haven't you had enough?'

'Not nearly enough,' he growled roughly. 'And what could possibly be wrong? I have my sweet loving wife beside me, the wife I love above everything else,' his eyes glittered dangerously. 'Even tennis, apparently.'

Her shoulder slumped defeatedly. 'You saw the newspapers.'

He nodded grimly. 'I also had half a dozen reporters on my tail asking for more information.'

'I'm sorry——'

'Sorry!' Nick repeated harshly. 'Why should you be sorry? No, I'm the one that's sorry, Rachel, sorry your little plan didn't work.'

She blinked dazedly. 'Plan? What plan? Anna Hill wanted to ask me a few questions——'

'Anna Hill?' he echoed sharply. 'Who the hell is Anna Hill?'

'The reporter——'

'You didn't tell me you had a friend who was a reporter,' his mouth twisted derisively.

'I haven't——'

'No?'

'No!'

Nick shrugged. 'It doesn't matter. It isn't going to work anyway.'

'What isn't?' she cried out her frustration.

'This ploy of yours to gain the interest of the public,' he rasped., 'I'm not going to feel in the least guilty about throwing you out of my life the moment I know I don't have to continue with this marriage.'

Rachel had gone very white. 'You really mean that?'

His expression was scornful. 'Oh yes.'

She licked her suddenly dry lips, her head going back. 'Then I might as well go and pack my things,' she told him stiffly.

Nick caught up with her at the door, and swung her round, his gaze searching on her face. 'Does that mean what I think it means?' he finally ground out.

'Yes,' she answered abruptly.

His hand on her arm was painful, but she didn't feel a thing, hurting too much inside to care about physical pain. 'How long have you known?' he demanded grimly.

'A couple of days.'

'Why the hell didn't you tell me?'

Because she hadn't wanted this to happen, had been holding on to him as long as she could possibly could, in the hope that he might come to care for her in return. This last week had told her that wasn't possible. 'You haven't been here to tell,' she said stiffly.

'No,' he acknowledged quietly. 'You're leaving, then?'

She looked up at him unflinchingly. 'That was the bargain, wasn't it?'

'Yes,' he agreed gruffly.

'And as you don't like to say goodbye I'll say it for you. Goodbye, Nick.' Somehow her voice remained cool, revealing none of the choking emotion inside her.

'Rachel——'

'Goodbye,' she repeated hardly, quietly closing the door as she left.

CHAPTER EIGHT

THE young woman walking confidently along the high street, her head held high, bore little resemblance to the girl who had left Nick's apartment like a whipped puppy almost two years ago. She had matured almost beyond recognition; there was a happy glow in her eyes, a smile on her lips, her step was light and carefree.

Time has a way of erasing pain, of replacing one love with another, not erasing the first love, but certainly dulling it. That was what Matthew had done to Rachel's life. He had given her purpose again when the whole world seemed to have gone crazy.

'Everything all right, Hilary?' she asked the girl behind the counter of the bookshop as she went in.

'Fine.' The other girl picked up her handbag ready to go to her own lunch-break. 'He hasn't stirred.'

Rachel nodded. 'I'll see you later.'

She sat down behind the counter, looking down indulgently into the reclining push-chair that was serving as a bed for her son's lunchtime nap. At fourteen months Matthew was a big boy for his age, tall and lean like his father, with hair the colour of sunshine and eyes a deep stormy grey. Like most babies he had been tactful enough to include characteristics from both parents.

Nick would have been proud of his son—if he had known of his existence! Which he didn't.

Matthew was the reason Rachel had left Nick, the reason she had *had* to leave him. Maybe if he had seemed to be coming to care for her she would have stayed and hoped for the best, but those last heated words had shown her exactly what he thought of her.

She didn't happen to agree with Nick's opinion that a child, any child, needed both its parents. With Nick hating her, and her loving him, their child would have grown up in a battlefield.

And so she had left, had done the only thing possible in the circumstances. She couldn't pretend the last two years had been easy, they hadn't, but with her parents' help, both emotionally and financially, she had got through it. A few months ago her father had helped her finance a half share in this bookshop with Hilary. It wasn't exactly the sort of business they had once thought of running, but it was a start.

Her parents had been wonderful, taking care of Matthew when the shop was first opened, helping her through the first six months of his birth. She had paid her father's loan back now, but she knew she could still rely on them completely.

She had heard nothing from Nick, and she made no effort to contact him either, feeling he had no part of their lives now. She occasionally saw items about him in the newspapers, especially the blaze of publicity that had greeted his retirement after his spectacular win at Wimbledon last year.

She hadn't wanted to watch the match on television, but in the end she had been unable to stop herself. Nick had played like a demon, his concentration intense, his expression grim.

Her heart had given a sickening jolt at the sight of him, but she remained calm in front of her parents. It was only when she got to the privacy of the bedroom she shared with Matthew that she had allowed her tears to flow.

Suzy Freeman had been among the spectators, with her father, and as she moved her hand to straighten her hair, a huge diamond ring sparkled on the third finger. As she and Nick were still married she knew he couldn't possibly have married the other girl, but the ring on her finger showed that he had officially staked his claim.

Since his retirement Rachel had heard little about him. Until yesterday. Yesterday evening a photograph of him and a rapidly rising tennis star had appeared on the sports section of the news. It seemed Nick was the younger man's coach, and that he was bringing him over to Wimbledon with high hopes of him winning.

Her parents had looked at her rather anxiously as the newscaster passed on to something else, and she had steeled herself to show no emotion, excusing herself a short time later to go to the privacy of her bedroom. Matthew lay upside down in his cot, the sheet that had been his only covering in the hot June weather thrown to the floor before he fell asleep.

He looked so angelic as he slept on, completely unlike the mischievous little imp he was during the day, his still-baby face chubby and cute, and Rachel was rather proud of the eight teeth he had developed rather late in his young life. He was dressed in light blue pyjamas patterned with little brown teddy-bears, his hands stretched out star-like in his deep sleep, his blond curls giving him even more the look of an angel.

It was as she looked at Matthew that Rachel knew the last two years without Nick had been worth it. Matthew had so far grown up in a world of love, his grandparents adoring him, and her own love for him surpassed everything else, even her love for Nick. As a result Matthew was a happy, contented child, full of mischief, with a smile guaranteed to soften even the hardest heart. How would he have fared in the love-hate relationship of his parents, love on her side, hate on Nick's? Every time she asked herself that, and she did it a lot, the answer always told her that she had done the right thing, the only thing.

'Letter for you, love,' her mother told her when she arrived home later that evening, the chuckling Matthew going into his eager grandmother's arms while his mother opened her letter.

It was an invitation, to a birthday party—Eve Lennox's birthday party.

'Anything interesting?' Her mother looked concernedly into her pale face.

'No, nothing,' she replied brightly, screwing the invitation into a ball before throwing it into the bin.

Kay Lennox had made several attempts to see her since her break-up with Nick, and each time she had rebuffed the other woman, mainly out of necessity. She could hardly keep her baby a secret when she was six or eight months pregnant.

For a while after her first half a dozen refusals she had heard nothing from Kay, then had come the telephone call from the other woman asking her to be a godmother to little Eve. That refusal had been the hardest to make, but in the last months of her pregnancy she could hardly see Nick's sister. Besides, she had a feeling Nick himself would be there, would possibly even be a godfather, which was all the more reason to refuse.

A few weeks after the christening she had received an invitation to Eve's first birthday party. This invitation had gone unacknowledged; she had decided that if Kay were to get the hint to leave her alone that the break would have to be a clean one.

Like her break from Nick. She had heard nothing from him in two years, she hadn't expected to, and she hadn't been disappointed. She was hurt, and felt betrayed, but not disappointed.

For months after their separation she had lived in hope that Nick would miss her, that he would realise that he did love her after all. As the months passed and she heard no word from him she knew her hopes were in vain, and seeing him at Wimbledon last year, the way Suzy had congratulated him afterwards, had convinced her of it.

And now there was Kay's invitation! Nick on television yesterday, an invitation to Eve's party next would— would she never be rid of the St Clares from her life!

Not while she remained one herself! Maybe divorce was the only answer but so far she had heard nothing from Nick on the subject, and she was loathe to make the final break herself. Besides, there was always the chance that if she and Nick met in a courtroom Matthew's existence would come to light. No, it was better to leave it this way, to be a forgotten part of Nick's life.

Nevertheless, her unease deepened with the opening of Wimbledon, and she feared that at any moment Nick would come knocking on the door. Matthew, like most babies, was able to sense his mother's preoccupation, and instantly began having a series of minor accidents, the last one resulting in a slight concussion, stitches in the back of his head, and a night in hospital.

Rachel stayed with him as late as she could, not wanting to leave him. She had never been without him for a night before, although Matthew seemed to have no qualms, falling asleep at his normal time, and looking set to sleep through to the morning. It was at times like this that she wished she had the support of her husband, although as usual her parents were wonderful, only leaving the hospital an hour before she did.

The tears streamed down her face as she drove home, determined to be back at the hospital in the morning before Matthew had time to wake at his usual eight o'clock. Her eyes were watery, her nose red from crying when she entered the house at nine-thirty, with no premonition of the shock that awaited her.

Her mother came out of the lounge to meet her, frowning worriedly. 'Everything's all right, isn't it? Matthew——'

'Still fast asleep,' Rachel hastily reassured her. 'It's just—Oh, Mum, I do miss him!' She fell sobbing in her mother's arms.

'I think I've called at the wrong time,' drawled a deep familiar voice, a voice from the past.

Rachel raised a white face to look at her husband, her breathing shallow as she took in everything about him, from the overlong blond hair and grim face, to the brown trousers and shirt he wore; he was still in the peak of physical fitness, by the look of him.

He shrugged. 'I'll call back some other time——'

'No! I mean—Why are you here?' she demanded.

'Take Nick into the lounge, Rachel,' her father instructed. 'Your mother and I will be in the sitting-room.'

'Oh, but——'

'Come on, Dorothy,' he insisted as she protested.

'Rachel?' Her mother still lingered.

She licked her suddenly dry lips, conscious of the mess she must look to this man who so appreciated beautiful women. Her hair was worn in a bun at her nape for going to work, her blouse and skirt were smart rather than attractive, her face blotchy from her recent tears. But why should she feel so selfconscious about her appearance? Nick had no right to be here, none at all.

'I'll be fine,' she told her mother. 'Would you like to come this way?' she said to Nick in a hard voice.

He followed her through to the lounge, his expression grave. 'I haven't called at a good time,' he repeated huskily.

Rachel forced herself not to show even by a flicker of an eyelid that his being here disturbed her. 'What makes you think any time you called would be a good time? In fact, why have you called at all?' she asked tautly.

He shrugged. 'I was in London——'

Rachel nodded. 'At Wimbledon—I know.'

His eyes narrowed. 'You do?'

'The famous coach of Johnny Franks,' she derided. 'Of course I knew.'

'I thought I'd come and see you——'

'Why?'

'You've changed, Rachel,' he frowned. 'Grown harder.'

She looked at him unflinchingly, although the criticism hurt. 'We all change.'

'Yes. I've changed too, Rachel,' he added softly.

'Really?' her voice was cold with uninterest.

He flushed. 'I like to think so. I'm not quite so inflated with my own importance any more. You'll admit that was part of the trouble with our marriage?'

'Was it?'

'Yes,' he continued, despite her coldness. 'For instance, I've had time to think of the way we married, the reason we married.'

Her mouth twisted. 'I should think two years is long enough to think of that, yes,' she derided.

'Rachel——'

'You aren't wanted here, Nick,' she interrupted abruptly. 'Not any more.'

His eyes were narrowed. 'Your parents know the real reason we were married?'

Considering their bewilderment at her refusal to return to her husband, even though she carried his child, she had thought it best to tell them everything. At first they had been shocked, then their anger had turned to disappointment that she had not had more faith in them, and anger at Nick for his high-handedness.

'Yes, they know,' she confirmed.

'I thought so,' he nodded. 'Their manner to me was cooler than usual,' he explained.

'What did you expect?' Rachel snapped. 'The red carpet?'

'Hardly,' Nick drawled. 'Am I allowed to sit down?' he mocked.

'Please yourself,' she said ungraciously.

His expression mocked her as he relaxed in one of the armchairs. 'Why don't you sit down too?' he suggested softly.

'I prefer to stand.'

'So I see,' he sighed. 'Today was Eve's birthday,' he suddenly changed the subject.

'I know.'

'Kay said she invited you.'

'She did,' Rachel nodded.

'But you didn't want to go?'

'Obviously not.'

'Because of me?'

'You?' She blinked her puzzlement.

'Obviously not because of me,' Nick derided. 'Kay was disappointed you didn't come.'

'I was busy.'

'Yes,' his mouth tightened. 'With Matthew.'

Her mouth suddenly went dry, her breathing seeming to stop completely. 'What do you know about Matthew?' she squeaked.

'Only what your parents told me,' Nick said harshly.

'Which was?'

'That you were visiting him in hospital. Just who is he, Rachel?'

She twisted her hands together nervously. Obviously her parents hadn't told him much at all about Matthew. 'He—He's a friend.' She faced Nick bravely.

He seemed to tense. 'How much of a friend?'

'A very good one.'

'I see,' he said tightly. 'Now I understand your parents' reluctance to talk about him.'

Rachel swallowed hard. 'You do?'

'Well, you are still my wife, and if this Matthew is your boy-friend . . .!'

'Yes,' she agreed dully, 'I see what you mean.'

'Is he very ill?' Nick rasped.

She shook her head. 'Just concussion.'

His mouth twisted. 'You seemed upset enough when you came in.'

Her eyes flashed. 'Of course I was—It was the shock,' she added more calmly, breathing heavily.

'You care for him a great deal?'

'Yes.'

'You love him?'

'Yes.'

'God . . .!' he groaned harshly.

'What did you expect, Nick?' she demanded rebelliously. 'That I just sleep with him?'

'And do you sleep with him?'

'Often,' she told him defiantly.

Nick seemed to pale, then he stood jerkily to his feet. 'Then there's nothing more to be said. I hope you'll be happy, Rachel.'

'I am.' She followed him to the door. 'And you, Nick, are you happy?' His expression was harsh, his eyes grim. 'What is happiness?'

'You mean you haven't discovered that yet?'

'Obviously you have,' he said abruptly. 'Goodbye.'

'You don't like goodbyes,' she reminded him with a catch in her voice.

'I don't seem to have any choice this time,' he said ruefully. 'I suppose you'll be wanting a divorce?'

'I hadn't thought about it . . .'

'You don't want to marry Matthew?'

'I never wanted to marry *anyone*!'

'No,' Nick acknowledged dully. 'Well, good luck. And if you do decide you want a divorce Kay will know where you can reach me.'

'I'll remember that.'

'And——'

'I thought you were leaving, Nick,' Rachel said pointedly.

'Yes, I am. God, I made some mistakes with you!' he groaned.

'Let's hope you make more of a success of your second marriage.'

'I——'

'Goodbye, Nick,' her voice was shrill. If he didn't leave in a minute she would start to scream, and if she started she doubted she would be able to stop. She was too tense, already verging on the hysterical, it wouldn't take much to trigger it off.

'I think I prefer goodnight,' he said.

'I prefer goodbye!'

Nick gave an abrupt nod before he went, leaving a shaking Rachel behind him.

Seeing Nick tonight had been the last thing she expected, and coming so recently after her fright over Matthew, it had completely unnerved her.

'Rachel?'

Her mother had come out into the hallway at the sound of the front door quietly closing, frowning anxiously at Rachel's pale face.

'Mum,' she acknowledged ruefully, moving to join her parents in the sitting-room.

'It was such a surprise, Rachel.' Her usually calm mother was definitely flustered. 'When we got back from the hospital he was sitting in his car waiting for us. He wanted to know where you were. We were too shocked to prevaricate.'

'It's all right, Mum,' she soothed. 'As far as Nick is concerned Matthew is my boy-friend.'

'Is that wise?' her father frowned.

She shrugged. 'It was what he seemed to think, and what else could I say?'

'You could have tried the truth.'

'Jim!'

'Dad!' Rachel echoed her mother's cry of disbelief.

He stood up to pace the room. 'I never did like this deception of Nick.'

'He hasn't been here to deceive!' Rachel snapped.

'No . . .' he agreed slowly, 'there is that.'

'There's *only* that,' Rachel corrected. 'If he'd been at all interested in my welfare he would have been here when his son was born.'

'He didn't know about him.'

'He should have been here anyway!'

Her father's expression softened at her vehemence. 'You still love him.'

'No, I——'

'I've always admired your honesty, Rachel,' he said softly. 'It would be a pity to ruin it now.'

She flushed. 'I may still love him, I don't know. But what good did it ever do me?'

'It gave you Matthew.'

'Yes,' she agreed huskily. 'Oh yes,' her eyes glowed. Her small son was the very pinnacle of her existence.

'Why was Nick here?' her father asked softly.

'Why . . .?'

'Yes,' he nodded. 'What did he want?'

She looked perplexed. 'I—well, I—I don't know,' she finally admitted. 'I asked him that, and he said he came to see me, but . . . He did mention the fact that I hadn't been to Eve's birthday party,' she added lamely.

'That's a pretty feeble excuse for a man of Nick's intelligence,' her father derided.

'If he'd had any intelligence,' her mother said waspishly, 'he would have loved our Rachel. I'm inclined to think the man's a fool!'

'Oh, Mum!' Rachel gave an amused laugh, feeling her tension easing.

'Well . . .' her mother looked sheepish.

'I think you could be biased, Mum,' she teased.

'Maybe,' her mother conceded, smiling herself now.

'Definitely,' Rachel's father agreed dryly. 'I'm as aware of Rachel's good qualities as the next man, but you can't force love. If it isn't there then it isn't there.'

'No,' Rachel said dully. 'Nick said I could have a divorce any time I want one.'

'And do you want one?' her father asked softly.

'I don't know. I'll have to think about it.'

'Well, take your time,' he advised gruffly. 'Divorce is a big step, and it's usually final.'

She knew that, which was the reason she hesitated. 'Don't worry, Dad,' she assured him. 'I'm not going to rush into anything, not this time.'

She was aware as she lay in bed that night, Matthew's cot painfully empty beside her, that if it came to a divorce between her and Nick, it could be like this for all time. If Nick ever found out about Matthew, unlike his own father, he would fight *for* custody of his son, and if he won . . .! She couldn't even begin to think about life without Matthew!

CHAPTER NINE

MATTHEW was his usual cheerful self the next morning when she got to the hospital, seemingly not having missed her at all, as the nurse washed and changed him for the start of the day. Until he saw his mother, when he promptly burst into tears.

'Mummy, Mummy!' His arms came out to her pleadingly.

What mother could resist that woebegone tear-stained face? Certainly not Rachel. She scooped her small son up into her arms, crying herself after the night's separation from him.

The young nurse looked on indulgently. 'I'll leave you to finish dressing him, shall I?'

Rachel nodded. 'I've brought some of his own clothes with me.'

Matthew soon calmed down now that he had his mother with him, taking her round the ward to show her all the toys there that he didn't have at home.

Rachel laughed, 'We'll have to see what Father Christmas brings.'

He looked up interestedly at these new words. 'Faffer Christas?' he repeated curiously.

'Yes, darling,' she hugged him. 'Soon.'

'Soon,' he nodded eagerly. 'Now?'

'Soon,' she repeated firmly.

When Matthew came home from the hospital later that day Father Christmas had called six months early; the building bricks, fire engine, and farm animals he had so admired were waiting for him in neatly wrapped up parcels. The pleasure on his face as he demolished each wrapping to reveal the gifts was worth all the frantic searching through the shops for exactly the right toys.

Hilary arrived later that evening with a toy car for him. 'And how's my big brave man today?' she cuddled him.

'Spoilt,' Rachel grimaced. 'We're all so glad to have him home we're falling over each other to grant his least little request. Mum and Dad have been fussing over him so much that I've sent them to the cinema before they spoil him completely.'

'He deserves to be spoilt,' Hilary defended. 'Don't you, lamb?' She sat Matthew on her knee while she helped him get the car out of the box. 'How's your head, poppet?' she asked him.

'Hurts,' he pouted up at her with his cherubic face.

Rachel chuckled softly. 'Much more of this and I'll enter him for an Oscar!'

Hilary laughed too as Matthew 'brrm-brrmed' all around the room with his new car. 'He seems fine,' she commented.

'He is,' Rachel nodded. 'No damage at all, the doctor said.'

'I still feel so responsible. If I hadn't put those boxes there——'

'And if Matthew hadn't been disobedient and climbed them,' Rachel interrupted firmly, 'then he wouldn't have fallen off and cut his head.'

'No, but——'

'No buts, Hilary,' she insisted. 'If it was anyone's fault it was mine, for not watching him closely enough.'

Hilary went and sat down in an armchair as Matthew played happily on the floor with his new toys. 'Rachel,' she began hesitantly, biting down on her lips awkwardly, 'About this accident——'

Rachel sighed. 'I know exactly what you're going to say. I've already discussed it with my parents, and my mother has agreed to take care of Matthew for the mornings at least.'

Her friend nodded. 'That's something. I didn't like bringing it up, but since Matthew began walking a couple of months ago——'

'The accidents have been increasing,' Rachel acknowledged. 'The chaos too. But other than putting Matthew into a nursery all day, which I refuse to do, I don't see what can be done about it.'

'You wouldn't ask Nick for help? He's in town——'

'I know,' Rachel said tightly, not completely over the meeting with him yesterday.

'I'm sure if you asked him——'

'I couldn't,' she shook her head. 'You know I couldn't.'

'Matthew would be better if you stayed at home with him——'

'Utopia!' she derided. 'You know I can't do that. There isn't enough money for me to pay someone to take my place, and you can't run the place on your own.'

Hilary took a deep breath. 'Geoff asked me to marry him last night.'

'Oh, that's wonderful!' Rachel exclaimed excitedly. Hilary had been dating Geoff Crawford, the manager of a neighbouring shop, for the last six months, and the news of their engagement was thrilling. 'I hope you said yes,' she teased.

'Of course,' her friend smiled. 'I'm mad about him. But what I really wanted to tell you was this—if you want to get out of the shop. Geoff might be interested in buying your half from you.'

'He would?' Rachel's eyes widened, widening even more at the sum Hilary mentioned he might buy it for. 'Does he have that sort of money?'

'Well, Geoff is ten years older than me, and he's been saving for years for his own business. This would be ideal.'

The idea came as a complete surprise to Rachel. 'I— Can I think about it?'

'Of course,' Hilary laughed. 'I didn't expect a decision on it today. But it would seem to solve a lot of problems.'

As Hilary said, it would solve a lot of problems, not least being the guilt she had felt lately about leaving the responsibility of the shop more and more on Hilary's shoulders. Not that she thought Hilary begrudged her this time she was spending with Matthew, Hilary was too fond of Matthew herself to feel that way, but that didn't lessen her own feelings of guilt.

'Don't worry about it,' Hilary said at her frown. 'Geoff and I are in no hurry. We haven't even set a date for the wedding yet.'

'Don't forget to invite me,' Rachel teased.

'Are you kidding—I want Matthew to be my pageboy!'

'That I have to see,' Rachel said dryly.

'And me,' her friend giggled. 'Well, I'd better be off now, I'm meeting Geoff later. I only really came round to make sure my little man was all right.'

'Thanks!'

Hilary swung Matthew up into her arms. 'Well, it's true. If this handsome devil were a few years older I'd be marrying him instead of Geoff. And talking of handsome devils . . .'

'Which we weren't,' Rachel said firmly, knowing exactly what direction this conversation were taking, *who* it was leading to.

'I'll tell Geoff you said that, I'm sure he'll be flattered!'

'Oh, I didn't mean——'

'I know,' Hilary giggled at her consternation.

'Congratulate him for me, hmm?' Rachel took Matthew into her own arms. 'Bed for you, young man.'

'Car!' He held out his hand for it.

'All right, monster,' she laughed, picking it up for him, looking over at Hilary. 'When I've put all the toys in the cot that he wants to take to bed with him there won't be room for him!'

By the time she had fed and bathed Matthew, put him to bed, read him a story, and left him safely tucked up in his cot, it was too late to do anything other than collapse into an armchair.

It had been another hectic day, not least having Matthew safely home with her. And then there was Hilary's startling suggestion.

She had known for some time that something would have to be done about the situation. When her father had suggested helping her go into business Matthew had only been a small baby, but he had brought his walking to a fine art now, could seemingly move with the speed of light, and the mischief he had been getting into lately was becoming more and more serious.

Hilary's idea seemed to be the only way out, and yet Rachel was loath in a way to part with her independence. But Matthew came first, had always come first, and she knew she would make whatever decision was best for him.

Two faces appeared momentarily on the screen in front of her, two faces she knew achingly well—Nick and Suzy! Johnny Franks' picture had appeared now, and she turned up the volume to hear what the news-caster was saying about them.

'Mr Franks, who today won his way through to the semi-finals, is also said to be in a serious condition. Now on to the weather,' he said with a sudden change of topic.

Also said to be in a serious condition? What did that mean? Had Nick been hurt in some way? How could she find out that important part of the news she had missed?

Ring the television company? No, that was ridiculous, besides bordering on hysteria. *Kay* would know if Nick were injured.

There was no answer to her call. Why, Kay could be at the hospital with Nick right now, he could be—— No, she wouldn't think about it. Call the hospitals, that was the answer, call every one until she found the right one.

Her parents walked in as she was in the middle of a rather heated argument with another Emergency receptionist who said she wasn't at liberty to give out information on patients, not even their name. Rachel finally slammed the telephone down in disgust.

'Bureaucrat!' she snapped, glaring angrily at the inanimate telephone receiver.

'What on earth is going on?' her mother wanted to know.

'I'm trying to find out if Nick's dead or dying, and——'

'Dead . . .?' her mother echoed faintly.

Rachel's expression was frantic. 'He's been involved in an accident, and I can't seem to find out where he is, whether he's been badly injured—nothing!'

'Now calm down, darling,' her father soothed, 'and explain this to us reasonably.'

'Well, you see, it was on the news, and I missed it, but Nick was on there, and I——'

'I said reasonably, Rachel,' he encouraged. 'Reasonably.'

She took a deep breath, trying to be more lucid this time. 'I don't know what to do,' she choked.

'Well, you can stop worrying, for one thing,' her father told her briskly. 'Nick wasn't even in the car.'

'But——'

'We heard it on the radio driving home, Rachel,' her mother told her with obvious relief. 'Nick wasn't involved, but Mr Franks and his fiancée were.'

The world seemed to sway dizzily, and it took all her will-power to stop falling on to the floor in a dead faint. 'Nick is—all right?' she questioned hollowly.

'Yes,' her father nodded.

'Oh!' Her complete panic now seemed ridiculous, and the hot colour flooded her cheeks. 'I didn't hear it properly. I just assumed—How silly of me,' she gave a falsely bright smile.

'Not silly at all,' her mother said calmly. 'After all, Nick is Matthew's father.'

'Er—yes. I think I'll go to bed now, it's been a long day, one way and another,' she derided.

'Of course, Rachel.' Her mother kissed her goodnight.

'I'm just about to make some hot chocolate,' her father told her. 'I'll bring you a cup, shall I?'

'That would be lovely,' she accepted warmly, knowing she was too confused to go to sleep just yet. 'Matthew was fast asleep when I checked up on him a few minutes ago.'

Her father smiled indulgently. 'And we all know that once he's asleep he won't wake until morning, not even if the house were to fall down around him!'

Rachel had washed and changed into her night-clothes, and was reading by the small bedside lamp when her father came in with the hot chocolate. Matthew's cot was over in the darkened corner of the room.

'Here you are.' Her father sat down on the side of the bed, obviously having no intention of leaving just yet.

'Thanks.' She sat up to drink it. 'Good film?'

He shrugged. 'If you've seen one sci-fi you've seen them all—the more recent ones, that is. Still, it was a night out, and your mother enjoyed it.'

'Hilary came round this evening.'

'How is she?' he smiled. 'We haven't seen much of her lately, too busy with Geoff, I suppose?' he teased.

'Actually they've decided to get married.' She went on to tell him of the other couple's suggestion that they buy her half of the shop.

Her father's expression remained noncommittal. 'Do you want to sell?'

Rachel shrugged. 'I can't see any other way out of it. Matthew needs more and more of my attention, and I feel guilty for not giving him it. You and Mum are marvellous, but——'

'But we aren't his mother,' he nodded understandingly. 'Or his father either,' he added softly, watching her reaction.

She instantly stiffened. 'What do you mean?'

'Your mother and I have been having a chat tonight about Nick's visit yesterday.'

'I thought you went to the cinema!' Rachel played for time, sure she wasn't going to like what her father would say next.

'Don't try and change the subject, Rachel,' he chided. 'Seeing Nick again, talking to him, made us wonder if perhaps we hadn't been a little unfair keeping Matthew's existence from him.'

'Unfair——!'

'Yes,' he sighed. 'No matter what your mother's and my views on *why* the two of you got married are, Nick is Matthew's father——'

'And I'm his mother! And it would be disastrous if Nick knew about Matthew. He'd take him away from me, Dad,' she added pleadingly.

'Or the two of you would get back together,' he said softly.

'Which would be even more disastrous,' she said heatedly. 'Dad, you can't be serious about this?'

'You've already admitted that you still love him.'

'Precisely the reason I couldn't live with him again.'

'We aren't just thinking of you, Rachel. Matthew——'

'He's happy! You can't deny that he's happy,' Rachel said desperately.

'Because he's never known anything else. Matthew needs the love of both his parents, needs to have a father like other children. He isn't old enough to realise he's different yet, but when he does . . .' her father gave a pointed shrug. 'And have you thought about when he's older, when he realises that Nick is his father, and that you've kept the two of them apart? He may want to go to Nick then, anyway.'

'No . . .'

'It has to be faced, Rachel, Nick is rich and well-known. He can give Matthew more than you can——'

'He can't love him any more than I do!'

'You think not?' her father raised his brows. 'I think Nick has a great capacity for loving, especially where a child is concerned. It would be better if you gave Matthew the love and stability he needs now.'

'Together?'

'Yes.'

'You think Nick and I could do that?'

Her father stood up. 'Stop thinking of yourself, Rachel,' he told her bluntly. 'And try thinking of what Matthew needs.' He quietly left the room.

Her father's words might have been a little harsh, but she knew he was only doing it for her own good. And she could no longer deceive herself into believing that she had left Nick for her unborn baby's sake, to protect it from Nick's distrust of her. Her reason then was the same as now, she couldn't bear to live with Nick knowing the only reason he tolerated her in his life was because of his son.

She was doing a stock inventory the next day, while Hilary was at lunch, when the bell over the door rang to tell her she had a customer.

'Just coming!' she called, putting her list down on the top shelf, turning to descend the ladder.

'No rush.'

She almost fell down the ladder as she recognised that voice, and looked down into Nick's deep blue eyes. What was he doing here?

'Steady!' His hands came out to grasp her upper arms as she reached the floor, selfconsciously straightening her skirt.

'Hello,' she greeted huskily, her cheeks coloured a delicate pink as she realised the expanse of leg she must have shown on her way down the ladder.

'Hi,' he smiled.

'Er—What can I do for you?'

He didn't seem to hear her, and looked about him appreciatively. 'This is quite a nice little place.'

'What did you expect, a slum?' she flashed, at once on the defensive.

He shook his head reproachfully. 'I didn't expect anything. I didn't even know you had a store until Kay told me.'

'Kay . . .?' Rachel frowned. 'I didn't know she knew either.'

Nick shrugged. 'Well, she did. How are you, Rachel?'

'The same as two days ago—well.'

'And Matthew, how is he?'

She gave him a sharp look. 'Are you really interested?' After all, he had no idea Matthew was his son.

'No,' he said harshly. 'Why the hell should I give a damn how the man is who sleeps with my wife?'

'Then why ask?' she snapped.

'An effort at conversation.'

'Why bother——'

'Rachel!'

'Okay,' she sighed. 'I'm sorry. Would you like a cup of coffee?'

Nick frowned. 'Don't you have to stay open?'

'I meant here,' she said impatiently. 'I have a kettle and a pot of instant in the back.'

'Oh.'

An unwilling smile lightened her features. 'Not what you're used to, hmm?' She remembered the percolated coffee he drank all day when he was at home.

'Instant coffee will be fine.'

'Sure?' she grimaced.

'Yes. I——' he broke off as Hilary came into the shop. 'Good afternoon,' he greeted huskily.

'Hello,' she returned shyly. 'I was sorry to hear about your tennis player.'

'Thanks,' he nodded gravely.

'I'm going in the back for lunch now, Hilary,' Rachel told her softly. 'If you should need me . . .'

'I'll holler,' Hilary grinned.

'Yes,' Rachel returned the smile, then took Nick through the store-room to the room she and Hilary used for their breaks. It was barely more than a cupboard, and she was uncomfortably aware of Nick in its confines.

'If you're at lunch maybe I could take you out to eat,' he suggested huskily.

'I——'

'I'm hungry even if you aren't. I've been at the hospital most of the night.'

'I—All right,' she decided. 'But I can only be an hour.'

In the end they had a meal in a local café, a crowded room not really conducive to personal conversations.

'I was sorry to hear about Johnny Franks too,' Rachel told Nick as they ate their meal.

Nick nodded. 'He's a good player. Or rather, he was.'

'Was?' she frowned.

'He broke both legs in the accident. I doubt he'll ever get back to professional tennis.'

'Oh no!'

'Yes,' he sighed. 'Luckily Suzy came off a little better—a broken arm, concussion, and a few cuts and bruises.'

'Suzy?' she echoed sharply.

Nick sipped his wine. 'You remember Suzy Freeman, don't you?'

'Of course,' she said stiffly.

'I think this accident may delay the wedding for a while.'

'Wedding? But we aren't divorced yet!' Rachel gasped.

Nick frowned, slowly lowering his glass to the table.

'Would you care to explain that remark?'

'How can you marry Suzy when we aren't divorced?' She was very pale in her shock.

'Marry Suzy . . .?' he repeated slowly. 'What makes you think I'm going to marry Suzy, for God's sake?' he rasped.

'You mean you aren't?' she said dazedly.

'Of course I damn—No,' he amended more calmly. 'I'm married to you.'

'Yes, but——'

'I think we should get out of here, Rachel. Will you come home with me so that we can talk?'

'Come—home, with you?'

'Yes. Will you?' His expression was intent.

'I—I can't. The shop——'

'Surely Hilary can manage for a while?'

'I'm not sure. Oh, not about Hilary. I'm not sure I should come to the apartment with you. I'm not sure we have anything left to say to each other.'

'You're wrong,' he shook his head. 'Rachel, I have to talk to you. Alone,' he added grimly as a woman on the next table turned to give them a curious glance. 'Please, Rachel,' he had grasped her hand across the table, 'just give me half an hour of your time. Is that too much to ask?'

It wasn't, he knew it wasn't, and after calling Hilary to tell her she would be late back Rachel allowed herself to be guided to Nick's car and driven to the home they used to share together.

'I can't be late back,' she warned him.

'Half an hour,' he promised. 'And then I'll drive you home. If you still want to go,' he added softly.

She gave him a sharp look. 'I'll want to go,' she snapped.

'Okay,' he nodded abruptly. 'I just want you to listen

to what I've got to say, then you can leave any time you want to. I won't try and stop you.'

'I never doubted that for a moment,' she said bitterly. 'Just as I never doubted that I would go when I want to. I have no intention of staying any longer than I have to.'

It felt strange to be back in the apartment, especially as by the time she got there she was beginning to wonder if she should have agreed to this, whether she were being wise to be alone with Nick like this.

'Drink?' he offered.

'Er—tea?'

'Sure,' he nodded, disappearing into the kitchen.

The apartment was exactly as she had left it, even down to the china ornaments she herself had put about the lounge. Everything was achingly familiar, especially the records they had often listened to in the evenings before spending a night making love.

'You haven't changed anything,' Rachel commented as Nick came back into the room with the tea.

He shrugged. 'I've hardly been here. Even before I retired I lived mainly in America.'

'Then why keep it?'

'In the hope—I still needed an English base,' he amended. 'Somewhere to stay when Johnny was playing in England.'

'It all looks—very neat.'

'I've had a cleaner come in once a week and check everything over.'

'Efficient.' She took the proffered cup of tea, biting her lip pensively. 'I—You were going to tell me about Suzy.'

He shook his head, lounging in the chair opposite her. 'You were going to tell me why you thought I was going to marry her. As far as I'm concerned all she is, all she's ever been, is Sam's daughter.'

'But just now you mentioned a wedding. And she wears a ring, I've seen it.'

'Is there anything to say I gave her that ring?'

'No. But—well, she's always with you! The two of you were sitting together at Wimbledon——'

'She wears Johnny's ring, Rachel,' he interrupted softly. 'It's their wedding that will have to be delayed.'

Rachel swallowed hard. 'I—I didn't know that.'

'Obviously, although it's been no secret. Would it have bothered you if I *had* been the prospective bridegroom?'

'I——'

'The truth, Rachel,' Nick prompted huskily. 'Tell me the truth.'

'Why should I?' she flashed.

'Because I love you. Because I've always loved you,' he stated calmly.

She hadn't heard right, she couldn't have done. 'Nick, did you just say——'

'That I love you?' he queried grimly. 'Yes, I said it. And I meant it.'

CHAPTER TEN

RACHEL stood up agitatedly, pacing the room, occasionally glancing at Nick as if to confirm that she hadn't gone insane. He couldn't love her, couldn't really have said that.

'I love you, Rachel,' he said again.

She went to speak, stopped herself, started again, and again fell silent. Whatever Nick was saying to her it couldn't be, I love you.

'Rachel, please just say something!' he rasped. 'Even if it's only, I hate you!'

'But I don't.' Her voice came out quivery and unsure.

'Don't what?' he pursued. 'Don't want to talk to me? Or don't hate me?'

She wetted her suddenly dry lips. 'I—I don't hate you.'

'That's something,' he grimaced.

'Could—could you tell me again? The bit about loving me.' She looked at him with bewildered eyes.

'I fell in love with you the night we met——'

'No,' she shook her head, 'that's asking me to believe too much.'

'But I did, Rachel.' Nick came over to grasp her arms. 'The moment you smiled at me I felt a jolt here,' he put a hand to his heart. 'I haven't felt normal since.'

'But you always acted as if you hated me.'

'Because I felt betrayed, let down. I—I thought you were like my mother.'

'And now?' she asked huskily.

His eyes darkened. 'Now I want to make love to you so badly I ache with needing you,' he groaned.

'Then make love to me.' She fell weakly into his arms. 'I need you so badly, Nick.'

'Rachel . . .!'

'You aren't going to deny me?' Tears shimmered in her eyes.

'Never again.' He strained her to him. 'I'm never going to let you leave me again.'

What followed was the most beautiful experience Rachel had ever known. Their lovemaking reached the very pinnacle of unity, a oneness that came from mutual love and mutual desire.

Afterwards she lay in Nick's arms, her head resting on his chest, their arms still around each other, as if they were afraid they would lose each other again.

'You love me too.' Nick's chest moved beneath her as he spoke.

'Yes,' she confirmed huskily.

'How long? How long have you loved me?'

'From the beginning, like you.'

He moved so that they were facing each other, frowning disbelievingly. 'Then why didn't you tell me? Show me?'

'Why didn't you?' she teased gently.

'Pride,' he sighed heavily. 'I loved you, and yet I mistrusted the emotion, and you along with it. When we met I knew I was deeply attracted to you, that I wanted to sleep with you, and that night, after I lost the semi-final, you made no objection when I said I wanted to spend the night with you.'

'I thought you just meant the evening.' Rachel blushed at her naïveté.

Nick's mouth quirked with amusement. 'You little baby!'

'Well, I wasn't to know,' she said indignatly. 'I wasn't used to dating sophisticated men who thought nothing of going to bed with a woman on such short acquaintance.'

'Shorter, sometimes,' he mocked.

'Boastful!'

'Honest,' he corrected softly. 'I haven't been a saint——'

'Oh, I know that!'

'But then I hadn't been Casanova either,' he said sternly. 'You came along with your sweetness and beauty, tempting me beyond endurance. I had no idea you were an innocent, I didn't think there were any left. Then when I made love to you and found you untouched——! My mind went off at a tangent. There was that boy you were with in the park, kissing you quite passionately, according to Kay——'

'Nick, I wasn't kissing Danny,' she insisted firmly. 'In fact I was trying to find some way to make him stop kissing *me* when I saw Kay needed help.'

'You don't have to tell me this——'

'But it's the truth. Really, Nick,' she looked at him pleadingly.

'Well, I wasn't to know that at the time,' he sighed. 'I took that fact, added to the way you responded to me, the way you didn't deny wanting to spend the night with me——'

'And decided I was trying to trick you in some way.'

'Yes,' he said tersely. 'With my background——'

'Which I had no knowledge of. I had no idea of the way your parents treated you, Nick,' she touched his cheek as if to take away the past pain. 'Or of your adoption. Suzy told me at the wedding.'

'The wedding?'

'Yes,' Rachel nodded. 'You know we went out into the garden together. Don't you remember, I told you we'd been talking about you?'

'And that was it?' he frowned. 'That's what you were talking about?'

'Yes. Suzy thought I ought to know the reason you hated me so much. Plus your own plans for a wedding,' she added questioningly.

'Suzy and me?' Nick exclaimed.

She swallowed hard. 'Wasn't it true?'

'Never,' he shook his head dazedly. 'But she told you it was?'

Rachel nodded. 'Plus all the hundreds of times she could have trapped you into marriage the same way.'

'You told her the reason we were getting married?'

'No, you did,' she frowned.

'No,' he denied huskily, 'I didn't tell anyone. Maybe she guessed?'

'It isn't the sort of thing you would just guess!' she scorned. 'You must have told her, Nick.'

'No,' he insisted. 'Maybe she tried a long shot and you fell for it? Suzy can be a devious little cat when she wants to be.'

Looking back on the conversation, Rachel realised she could have told Suzy more than she actually knew, could have fallen into a trap, as Nick said. One thing was sure, she believed Nick when he said he hadn't told the other woman.

'But you did sleep with her when you went away to play tennis,' she said with remembered pain.

'I've never slept with Suzy,' he rasped. 'And certainly not when I was away playing tennis. I was married to you.'

Rachel frowned. 'But that time you telephoned me

she asked you if you were ready to go to dinner. You even made your call to me in front of her!'

'I was in the bedroom——'

'That just makes it worse!' she choked.

'And Suzy and her father were in the lounge,' he explained gently. 'I had a suite, and I went into the bedroom to call you while they waited for me. Was she the reason you wouldn't join me in Canada?' he frowned suddenly.

'Yes.'

He gave a deep sigh. 'I'm beginning to think I may have underestimated Suzy all these years. She certainly seems to have been behind a lot of our troubles.'

'I think our mistrust of each other was behind that,' Rachel said ruefully.

'Maybe, but Suzy helped things along a bit. Was it you who told the newspaper about our marriage?'

'I talked to the reporter, but someone else had already told her about us.'

'And as Suzy was the one who put the seed of doubt in my mind I would hazard a guess that she was the one who put the word out. When I found out about the newspaper story I was so damned mad——'

'I noticed,' she grimaced.

'I thought you were tricking me like my mother tricked my father. I wanted you with me in Canada because I couldn't play for thinking of you, I thought you were really coming to care for me, and then that story appeared...! I could have strangled you!' Nick groaned. 'The worst of it was, it was all true. You were more important to me than tennis, than anything, and being without you was agony.'

'You could have taken me with you.' Rachel played with the glistening golden hair on his chest.

'When I left I didn't think it was a good idea, I

found it hard to keep my hands off you at the best of times,' he admitted huskily. 'But being away from you was worse the second time. By the end of the first week I was climbing the wall. My tennis was appalling!'

'Why did you decide to come and see me now, Nick? Why now? It's been two years.'

'God, don't I know it! I thought maybe by now you might have forgiven me.' He gently caressed her thigh as they talked.

'For what?'

'For telling you to get out of my life. I didn't really mean it. But we're back together now,' his arms tightened about her. 'I can hardly believe it.'

Neither could Rachel. She had never thought they could be so happy, not even in her wildest imaginings. And it was going to go on and on . . .

'The first thing you have to do is tell this Matthew things are over between you,' Nick continued. 'I can't say I like the idea of your having slept with another man, but that's in the past now. I was no angel before I met you, and you're a lot younger than me—What's wrong? Where are you going?' he groaned as she sat up in the bed.

Matthew! Heavens, she had forgotten all about Matthew—Nick's son. *Her* son. What was Nick going to do when he knew they had a child, a child she had kept hidden from him for two years? Her happiness suddenly seemed a frail thing.

'Rachel, I'm not angry.' He swung out of bed, pulling on a robe to come over to where she was frantically pulling on her clothes. 'We were separated, you were free to sleep with whoever you want to.'

Rachel looked up at him with pained eyes. 'Did you?'

'No one,' his eyes were gentle. 'No one at all. But I

don't condemn you. I just want you to finish with this Matthew and——'

'I can't,' she choked, straightening. 'I can't ever give him up. You see——'

'You can't mean that,' Nick gasped. 'Rachel, you can't want us both!'

'But I do. You see——'

'For God's sake don't say any more.' He was very pale. 'You love him, is that it?'

'Yes.'

'But you just said you love me,' he groaned.

'I do——'

'Hell, you can't love us both, want us both!'

'But I do. Nick, just let me explain——'

'I don't want to know!' He thrust her away from him. 'I have to get myself a drink,' he muttered, turning to leave the room.

'Nick——'

'Get out, Rachel,' he ordered harshly. 'And this time I never want to see you again.'

'Nick——'

'Ever!' he shouted vehemently, and slammed out of the room.

Rachel trembled at his anger. She had handled this badly, so badly, and now there seemed only one thing left to do.

She left quietly, the chink of glass in the lounge telling her that Nick was still drinking. She hoped he wouldn't be too drunk to listen to her when she got back.

Matthew had spent the day with her mother because of his accident, and he was still asleep from his nap when she got home, delaying her return to Nick's apartment. One thing guaranteed to put Matthew in a bad mood was a forced wakening from his nap, and she wanted him his usual sunny self when he met his father for the first time.

'Anything wrong, dear?' her mother asked as Rachel paced the room waiting for Matthew to wake.

She felt a little embarrassed as she told her mother what had happened that afternoon, although she could tell her mother wholeheartedly approved of the fact that she and Nick were, she hoped, getting back together.

'If he can forgive me for Matthew,' she added anxiously.

'Forgive you?' Her mother raised her eyebrows. 'The silly man made it impossible for you to stay with him!'

'Yes,' Rachel agreed ruefully. 'I think I heard Matthew,' she brightened.

'So did I,' her mother nodded. 'I——' the doorbell rang. 'You answer the door, I'll see to Matthew.'

'But——'

'Go along, dear. I'll give Matthew a drink while you get ready to go out.'

Rachel was frowning as she opened the door, but the frown soon turned to a gasp of amazement. 'Nick . . .!'

He was very pale, deep lines beside his nose and mouth—and surprisingly sober. 'Can I come in?' His voice was gruff.

'Of course.' She held the door open. 'I—Why are you here?'

'Because I knew you wouldn't come back,' he rasped. 'You can keep him, Rachel,' he told her abruptly, the strain he was under intense. 'If the only way I can keep you is by sharing you then that's what I'll do.'

She looked up into his proud face, knowing the effort his words cost him, tears flooding her eyes. 'Oh, Nick——'

'Don't pity me, Rachel,' he said tautly. 'And don't ever tell me anything about this Matthew. You can see him, but I don't want to know about it.'

'Nick, please,' she touched his arm. 'Come and meet Matthew.'

He tensed beneath her hand. 'You mean he's here?'

'With my mother,' she nodded.

'My God, you didn't waste much time!' His expression was grim.

'Please come and meet him, Nick,' she pulled him along with her. 'It isn't what you think.'

'For God's sake, Rachel——'

By this time she had him in the lounge, Matthew was playing on the carpeted floor on his own while her mother was preparing the chocolate milk shake he was so fond of.

'My God——!' Nick muttered dazedly. 'Rachel . . .?'

'Mummy! Mummy!' Matthew had turned and seen them, running into Rachel's waiting arms, hiding his face in her throat as he saw the stranger with her.

She heard Nick gasp at her side, and was terrified to look up, not knowing whether she would see condemnation or pleasure on his face. 'Yes, it's Mummy, darling,' she took the safe course and spoke to Matthew. 'Did you have a nice nap?'

Matthew had eyes only for Nick now. 'Man,' he announced proudly.

'Yes,' she gave a choked laugh.

'Rachel, is this—Can he be——'

'Let the man hold you, Matthew.' She held her son out to Nick.

For a moment Matthew hesitated, then he went eagerly into his father's arms, his shyness, as usual, not lasting long.

Nick looked down at him in dazed wonder, at eyes as grey as Rachel's, but the golden hair and features all his own. Matthew grinned at him as he investigated the recesses of his ear.

'Don't do that to Daddy, darling.' Rachel gently removed his fingers.

'My God, it is!' Nick choked.

Rachel still couldn't look at him, concentrating all her attention on Matthew. 'I said no, Matthew,' she repeated sternly. 'Daddy doesn't like his ears poked.'

'Daddy,' he repeated triumphantly.

'Very clever,' she gave a choked laugh. 'Clever boy, Matthew!'

'Dad-dy. Daddy,' he beamed.

'Oh dear, now what have we started?' she teased lightly.

Nick drew in a ragged breath. 'He's my son!'

'Yes,' she nodded, her eyes downcast.

'Why, Rachel? *Why?*'

She didn't pretend not to know what he meant, her eyes flashing as she looked up at him for the first time, a greyness to his skin now, a look of wonder in his eyes as he looked at Matthew, as he couldn't seem to take his eyes off him.

'I have my pride too, Nick,' she sighed. 'And I had no intention of staying with you once I knew I was pregnant. You see, I knew how much I loved you by that time, how much it would hurt me to be your wife on sufferance. I was wrong to deny you your son, I know that, it was completely selfish of me, but I——'

'If you were selfish so was I,' Nick stopped her condemnation mid-flow. 'Rachel, our child—Matthew,' he smiled down shakily at his son with love. 'Matthew could have been conceived after we were married,' he told her steadily.

'After . . .?' she repeated dazedly.

'My naïve little baby,' he chided gently, touching her cheek with loving fingers. 'You know nothing, do you? I didn't try to prevent a child between us, not before or after we were married.'

'I don't understand . . .' She shook her head in puzzlement.

'It's quite simple, Rachel. I *wanted* you to become pregnant, to keep you with me, to have you as my wife without admitting to the weakness of loving you. I had no idea that being pregnant by me was the one thing guaranteed to take you away from me.'

She swallowed hard. 'And how do you feel about loving me now? Do you still feel it's a weakness?' She held her breath as she waited for his answer.

Nick smiled, a warm loving smile that held back none of his emotions. 'With you at my side I could capture the world.' His voice was strong and commanding. 'With you *and* Matthew at my side I could capture the universe!' He was suddenly serious. 'Will you be at my side, both of you?'

'Daddy!' Matthew shouted once again, obviously feeling he had been ignored long enough.

Rachel gave a husky laugh. 'Well, he seems to have made his mind up.'

Nick's expression was content. 'And you—have you made your mind up?'

She gave him a clear untroubled smile. 'I never had a choice—and I never wanted one.'

'I love you,' Nick groaned.

'I love you too.'

'Later on tonight I'd like to show you how much,' he questioned.

She raised teasing eyebrows. 'I don't know how Matthew will feel about that. You see, up to now he's shared my room with me.'

'And you let me think——! You, Mrs St Clare, are not going to get any sleep tonight, you're going to be showing me how sorry you are for deceiving me,' he warned.

A loud cough from the hallway heralded her mother's entrance with Matthew's milk, obviously feeling she had waited in the kitchen long enough to give them the time they needed to sort things out between them. Matthew struggled to go down to the floor, drinking the milk shake down thirstily.

'Greedy little devil, isn't he?' Nick murmured proudly.

'Like his father,' she nodded absently. 'Nick——'

His hand grasped hers understandingly. 'This is a new beginning for us, Rachel. The past is forgotten. Yes?'

'Yes,' she agreed fervently.

'Only one thing hasn't changed, our love for each other, only this time we won't keep it hidden. And who knows,' he added teasingly, 'Matthew may be going to have a brother or sister because of this afternoon.'

'Not again!' Rachel groaned.

'I'd be with you this time, Rachel.' Nick's hand tightened painfully. 'From now on I'll always be with you.'

It was a promise for the future, and one Rachel readily accepted.

THE ORIGINS OF TENNIS

There is something terribly elegant and contemporary about the game of tennis—the players all dressed in white, the graceful swoop of their arms as they serve, the soft and rhythmic "thwack" of the ball as it is hit back and forth over the net. Yet the origins of the modern game go back hundreds of years.

Although ball-and-racket games were known to have been played in ancient Persia, Egypt, Greece and Rome, the game came into its golden age in sixteenth-century France. French kings built indoor tennis courts at their palaces, and there were 250 public courts in Paris alone. In 1598, an English visitor to Paris declared, "There be more tennis players in France than ale drinkers in England!" The name "tennis" derives from the French exclamation "tenez!" meaning literally, "take it!" or more broadly, "play ball!"—which is what players shouted at the beginning of games.

In the latter half of the nineteenth century an Englishman, Major Walter Wingfield, devised and patented a new outdoor court, and the game of lawn tennis quickly became popular in England. An American, Mary Outerbridge, is credited with spreading tennis to the United States after spending the winter of 1874 in Bermuda and watching British officers play. She returned to New York with a net, rackets and balls, and soon Americans were playing tennis, too.

The most famous and prestigious tennis tournament in the world today is, of course, at Wimbledon, a suburb of London. This tournament attracts as spectators not only the British royal family and the rich and famous from all over the world, but also thousands of ordinary people with one thing in common—a love for this elegant, yet thrilling star-studded game.

DISCOVER...

SUPERROMANCE

From the publisher that understands how you feel about love.

Almost 400 pages of outstanding romance reading in every book!

Take these 4 best-selling novels FREE

Yes! Four sophisticated, contemporary love stories by four world-famous authors of romance FREE, as your introduction to the Harlequin Presents subscription plan. Thrill to *Anne Mather*'s passionate story BORN OUT OF LOVE, set in the Caribbean.... Travel to darkest Africa in *Violet Winspear*'s TIME OF THE TEMPTRESS....Let *Charlotte Lamb* take you to the fascinating world of London's Fleet Street in MAN'S WORLD....Discover beautiful Greece in *Sally Wentworth*'s moving romance SAY HELLO TO YESTERDAY.

Harlequin Presents...

The very finest in romance fiction

Join the millions of avid Harlequin readers all over the world who delight in the magic of a really exciting novel. EIGHT great NEW titles published EACH MONTH! Each month you will get to know exciting, interesting, true-to-life people .... You'll be swept to distant lands you've dreamed of visiting .... Intrigue, adventure, romance, and the destiny of many lives will thrill you through each Harlequin Presents novel.

Get all the latest books before they're sold out!

As a Harlequin subscriber you actually receive your personal copies of the latest Presents novels immediately after they come off the press, so you're sure of getting all 8 each month.

Cancel your subscription whenever you wish!

You don't have to buy any minimum number of books. Whenever you decide to stop your subscription just let us know and we'll cancel all further shipments.

Your FREE gift includes

Anne Mather—Born out of Love
Violet Winspear—Time of the Temptress
Charlotte Lamb—Man's World
Sally Wentworth—Say Hello to Yesterday